Engaging Shaw

John Morogiello

with excerpts from
Bernard Shaw

D1523301

A SAMUEL FRENCH ACTING EDITION

FOUNDED 1830

SAMUELFRENCH.COM
SAMUELFRENCH-LONDON.CO.UK

ISBN 978-0-573-70149-8

www.SamuelFrench.com
www.SamuelFrench-London.co.uk

FOR PRODUCTION ENQUIRIES

UNITED STATES AND CANADA
Info@SamuelFrench.com
1-866-598-8449

UNITED KINGDOM AND EUROPE
Theatre@SamuelFrench-London.co.uk
020-7255-4302

Each title is subject to availability from Samuel French, depending upon country of performance. Please be aware that *ENGAGING SHAW* may not be licensed by Samuel French in your territory. Professional and amateur producers should contact the nearest Samuel French office or licensing partner to verify availability.

MUSIC USE NOTE

Licensees are solely responsible for obtaining formal written permission from copyright owners to use copyrighted music in the performance of this play and are strongly cautioned to do so. If no such permission is obtained by the licensee, then the licensee must use only original music that the licensee owns and controls. Licensees are solely responsible and liable for all music clearances and shall indemnify the copyright owners of the play(s) and their licensing agent, Samuel French, against any costs, expenses, losses and liabilities arising from the use of music by licensees. Please contact the appropriate music licensing authority in your territory for the rights to any incidental music.

IMPORTANT BILLING AND CREDIT REQUIREMENTS

If you have obtained performance rights to this title, please refer to your licensing agreement for important billing and credit requirements.

ENGAGING SHAW received its world premiere on August 20, 2006, at Oldcastle Theatre Company in Bennington, Vermont (Eric Peterson, Artistic Director). The performance was produced and directed by Langdon Brown, with sets and lights by Harry Feiner. The Stage Manager was Diane Healy. The cast was as follows:

SIDNEY WEBB.....................................Richard Howe
BEATRICE WEBB................................Gwendolyn Lewis
BERNARD SHAW..................................Mark Leydorf
CHARLOTTE PAYNE-TOWNSHEND................Katrina Ferguson

ENGAGING SHAW received its east coast premiere on March 15, 2008, at New Jersey Rep in Long Branch New Jersey (SuzAnne Barabas, Artistic Director, and Gabor Barabas, Executive Producer). The performance was directed by Langdon Brown, with sets by Charles Corcoran, lighting by Jill Nagle, costumes by Patricia Doherty, and sound by Merek Royce Press. The Production Stage Manager was Rose Riccardi. the cast was as follows:

SIDNEY WEBB.....................................Marc Geller
BEATRICE WEBB..................................Helen Mutch
BERNARD SHAW..................................Ames Adamson
CHARLOTTE PAYNE-TOWNSHEND................Katrina Ferguson

ENGAGING SHAW received its New York premiere on April 18, 2010, at Abingdon Theatre Company (Jan Buttram, Artistic Director). The performance was directed by Jackob G. Hofmann, with sets by The Ken Larson Company, costumes by Deborah J. Caney, lighting by Matthew McCarthy, and sound by Larry Spivack. The Production Stage Manager was Mickey McGuire. The cast was as follows:

SIDNEY WEBB.....................................Marc Geller
BEATRICE WEBB...........................Victoria Jamee Vance
BERNARD SHAW..................................Warren Kelley
CHARLOTTE PAYNE-TOWNSHEND...................Claire Warden

CHARACTERS

SIDNEY WEBB – 38-40. Energetic, short, working class accent, lisp.

BEATRICE WEBB – 38-40. Sidney's wife, upper class accent.

BERNARD SHAW – 40-42. An Irish music and drama critic who dabbles in playwriting.

CHARLOTTE PAYNE TOWNSHEND – 40-42. An heiress from Ireland.

AUTHOR'S NOTES

All quotations from the works and letters of Bernard Shaw are used by permission of the Society of Authors on behalf of the estate of Bernard Shaw.

Excerpts from "The Historic Basis of Socialism" by Sidney Webb are taken from *Fabian Essays on Socialism* published by the Fabian Society in 1889. They are used with permission of the publisher and the London School of Politics and Economics.

Excerpts from the diaries of Beatrice Webb are taken from a microform holograph of the original diary and the accompanying typescript published by Chadwyck-Healey in 1978. They are used with permission of the publisher and the London School of Politics and Economics.

ACT ONE

Scene 1

(A spotlight pierces the darkness and shines on Sidney **WEBB***, who appears to be speaking to a multitude.)*

WEBB. "How do we convince a man to sacrifice self for the needs of the community? Most socialist organizations in England would recommend force. But the Fabian Society rejects violence as a persuasive instrument, believing that the mainstream which has borne European society toward socialism during the past hundred years is the irresistible progress of *democracy.*"

(As he continues, the lights gradually come up to reveal the drawing room of a cottage in Stratford, where **WEBB** *has been practicing a speech he will give at a later date. His wife,* **BEATRICE***, sits at her desk, fretting over the bills.)*

"The progress of democracy means nothing less than a complete dissolution of the nexus by which society has been held together. This dissolution will be followed by a period of anarchic spiritual isolation of the individual from his fellows…"

BEATRICE. I can't think with you going on like that.

WEBB. I can't stop now, I've hit my stride. "But man is a social animal; and after more or less interval there will come into existence, not through violence but through gradualism and permeation, a new nexus, a *social* nexus, a *collective* nexus – "

BEATRICE. Oh, Sidney stop. I don't want to hear about nexuses when paying the bills.

(She looks at one, standing.)

BEATRICE. *(cont.)* Here's another: Slates. Twenty pounds, seven and six. Not to mention the lease on the building. What good is a school of economics that can't balance its own ledger?

*(**WEBB** sits at the other desk, revising his speech.)*

WEBB. Solicit another subscription from Miss Payne-Townshend when she arrives.

BEATRICE. I have bigger plans for Miss Payne-Townshend.

*(**SHAW** jovially storms in from the house, carrying three letters, two sealed, one open. **BEATRICE** moves closer to **WEBB**.)*

SHAW. Here's a damned fool! A publisher, who wants to foist my plays upon an unsuspecting populace to further the cause of socialism! Can you fathom the daring, the pluck, the outright idiocy of such a proposal?! He won't profit a shilling. I shall accept this man's offer; if only to teach him a lesson in bad economy and the redistribution of wealth.

WEBB. I take it the post has come?

*(**SHAW** hands Sidney the two sealed letters and dons his cap, preparing to exit. **BEATRICE** keeps Sidney between herself and **SHAW**.)*

SHAW. I must telegraph this poor, deluded soul immediately. Most enjoyment I've had in weeks!

*(**SHAW** storms off down left. **WEBB** reads the address on one of the sealed letters and calls **SHAW** back.)*

WEBB. I say, Shaw.

*(**SHAW** reenters. **WEBB** stands.)*

I seem to have got one of yours.

SHAW. Oh?

WEBB. From Miss Terry.

SHAW. Ah!

(SHAW takes the envelope from WEBB and inhales its perfume. WEBB crosses left. SHAW sits at his desk, places his cap down, and opens the letter. BEATRICE crosses to the other desk and sits.)

BEATRICE. What sort of a revolutionary writes love notes to actresses?

SHAW. An exceedingly happy one.

WEBB. Have you become a revolutionary? Must be the country air.

SHAW. Gradualism and permeation are still my tools. What's to overthrow? England is subject to a revolution with every new Prime Minister.

WEBB. Just the point I was making in my speech.

SHAW. The one with the period of anarchic spiritual isolation before social acceptance of the new nexus?

WEBB. The same. It's like getting married, really.

SHAW. Drivel!

WEBB. As a bachelor, you deny it.

SHAW. *(standing)* As a man of sense, I deny it.

WEBB. *(approaching SHAW)* But there will come a time, someday, suddenly, when you'll realize you're completely alone. At that point, even you will come to terms with the new arrangement and recognize that marriage is the perfect social model. One and one, when placed in a sufficiently integrated relationship, make not two, but eleven.

BEATRICE. Sidney, you're a poet.

(BEATRICE hugs WEBB.)

WEBB. Hm?

(BEATRICE kisses WEBB.)

Oh.

(BEATRICE kisses WEBB again with passion. SHAW continues as they kiss.)

SHAW. The acceptance of socialism is a *triumph*. It should not arise as the result of romantic loneliness and defeat, as you suggest.

(**SHAW** *is embarrassed.*)

Don't mind me.

(**SHAW** *picks up his cap from the desk.* **BEATRICE** *breaks the kiss.* **WEBB** *regains his breath.*)

BEATRICE. Are you going far?

SHAW. Riding down to the telegraph.

BEATRICE. Don't be long. I need you to be here when Graham Wallas and Miss Payne-Townshend arrive.

SHAW. Who?

WEBB. Charlotte Payne-Townshend. She attended a few of the general meetings.

SHAW. What did she look like?

BEATRICE. A large, graceful woman. Brown hair, gray eyes.

SHAW. Attractive?

WEBB. In her evening clothes she approaches beauty.

SHAW. (*Expressing interest. Putting down the cap.*) Does she?

BEATRICE. At moments she is plain.

SHAW. (*Uninterested. Grabbing the cap.*) No recollection.

BEATRICE. I am hoping that Miss Payne-Townshend will support the school.

SHAW. (*approaching* **BEATRICE**) And you would like me to chat with her and be utterly charming.

BEATRICE. (*holding Sidney's hand*) If at all possible.

(**SHAW** *crosses to the down left door and stops.*)

SHAW. Certainly it is possible. If she were to wear her evening clothes, it would be entirely *probable.*

(**SHAW** *dons the cap and exits waggishly.* **WEBB** *looks after him with admiration.*)

WEBB. What a dreadful philanderer he is.

(**WEBB** *sees* **BEATRICE** *and admiration fades. He sits and opens the other letter.*)

BEATRICE. He is a sprite. It is not the end he cares for, it is the process. He delights in being the candle to the moths. Dear Shaw may never accept the nexus of marriage.

WEBB. *(reading the letter)* Despite your best efforts.

BEATRICE. I beg your pardon?

(WEBB looks at BEATRICE, teasing her.)

WEBB. Don't play innocent. You have worked quite actively over the past few months to set Bertha Newcombe on Shaw's trail.

BEATRICE. *(crossing away from WEBB)* – Why not? She's painting another portrait. Shaw sits for her whenever he can spare a moment.

WEBB. Bertha devoting her life to painting Shaw certainly indicates affection for him. But Shaw devoting his life to being painted only indicates affection for himself.

BEATRICE. *(turning to WEBB)* He can't be indifferent to her feelings.

WEBB. The way he is with all the others? He exchanges letters with that actress every day. I've lost count of his other interested parties.

BEATRICE. I hope Shaw's not too charming with Miss Townshend. *(approaching WEBB with conspiratorial excitement)* I've got her down for Graham Wallas.

WEBB. Bo!

BEATRICE. Don't you think they would get along?

(WEBB stands, still holding the letter.)

WEBB. You must stop creating romantic discord among our circle. What are you thinking?

BEATRICE. *(grabbing a bill)* "Slates!" is what I am thinking! We need a benefactor. Miss Townshend was happy to oblige in the past, so...

(WEBB crosses away from her, still holding the letter.)

WEBB. So you thought you would make her a permanent benefactor by marrying her to Wallas.

BEATRICE. Marriage would solidify her conviction.

WEBB. *(reading the letter again)* Or provide her with no means of escape.

BEATRICE. Why shouldn't I lead our friends to the blissful partnership we experience? Especially when it will balance the books.

WEBB. I should know better than to argue against your romantic plots.

*(**WEBB** expects a kiss. Instead, **BEATRICE** pats his cheek and sits at the stage left desk.)*

BEATRICE. Yes, you should, dear boy.

WEBB. *(handing her the letter)* I'm glad to say we may not be here to witness the fruits of your labor. We've been invited to America.

BEATRICE. *(unconvincing)* A lecture tour? How nice.

SHAW. *(off in the distance)* Mind! MIND!!!

*(A woman's scream from offstage, down left, followed by a crash. **WEBB** and **BEATRICE** react over the following.)*

CHARLOTTE. My leg!

SHAW. Damn these country roads!

CHARLOTTE. Oh, my leg!

WEBB. Blast! Not again!

*(**SHAW** enters down left, carrying **CHARLOTTE**.)*

BEATRICE. What happened?

SHAW. I couldn't get around. She swerved off the road to avoid me and went screaming into the ditch.

WEBB. Is she hurt?

SHAW. What the devil do you think?

BEATRICE. Come over to the sofa.

*(**BEATRICE** clears a space on he sofa as **WEBB** assists **SHAW**.)*

CHARLOTTE. Gently, please.

BEATRICE. You and that bicycle will kill someone someday.

SHAW. You're disappointed it wasn't me.

(*They gently place* CHARLOTTE *onto the sofa.* SHAW, *to the left of the sofa, places a cushion beneath her foot.* WEBB *and* BEATRICE *stand above them superfluously.*)

SHAW. This leg?

CHARLOTTE. The calf.

SHAW. Is the skin broken?

(SHAW *lifts* CHARLOTTE*'s dress and begins to examine her leg in a medically professional and expedient manner.*)

BEATRICE. Should you really be doing that?

SHAW. Yes, perhaps I should pay heed to decorum and watch the woman suffer without attempting to assist. Merely bruised.

BEATRICE. (*crossing down*) I can assist her.

SHAW. Good, then. Vinegar and brown paper.

BEATRICE. What?

SHAW. Fetch some. It will reduce the swelling.

WEBB. I don't know that we have any.

(SHAW *rises, chasing the* WEBB*s off over the following.*)

SHAW. Then find some, dammit! Alert the neighbors! Wake the shopkeeper! Alleviate the woman's suffering!

(WEBB *and* BEATRICE *exit in haste down left.* CHARLOTTE *calls after them.*)

CHARLOTTE. A beefsteak will work just as well!

SHAW. (*turning to her*) My dear, we are not apt to find a beefsteak in a house full of vegetarians.

CHARLOTTE. You are a vegetarian?

(SHAW *crosses around her.*)

SHAW. Did you suppose I was in the habit of chewing the dead bodies of animals? Ugh! And yet I confess I once did it habitually, as recently as fifteen years ago; but not since then. Bernard Shaw. How do you do?

(He holds out his hand. She does not take it.)

CHARLOTTE. We've already met, Mr. Shaw. At a meeting of the Fabian Society. I mentioned at the time that I am particularly fond of the Quintessence of Ibsenism. The way Ibsen used his plays to expose the plight of women. It changed my life, actually.

(SHAW hangs his cap on the hook.)

SHAW. You must be Miss Payne-Townshend. The Webbs mentioned your arrival.

(SHAW moves a desk chair close beside her.)

They never told me you were Irish.

CHARLOTTE. From Derry.

(SHAW sits.)

SHAW. Any relation to the Dublin Townshends?

CHARLOTTE. That I am.

SHAW. I was an office boy for Uniacke Townshend, the land agent, many many years ago.

CHARLOTTE. How very interesting.

SHAW. It's the job I left to come down to London.

CHARLOTTE. What was the reason for your emigration?

SHAW. *(standing)* Same as yours, I suppose, or anyone's. As long as Ireland produces men who have the sense to leave her, she does not exist in vain.

CHARLOTTE. *(amused)* That's terrible.

SHAW. The truth always is. Shall I close you up, or shall we let it breathe?

CHARLOTTE. Like a fine wine.

(SHAW crosses away from her down right.)

SHAW. Your word will have to serve on that account. I am a teetotaler as well as a vegetarian.

CHARLOTTE. No wine? No meat? What do you do for enjoyment?

(He turns to her.)

SHAW. I call people fools. There's no greater enjoyment to be had. And you?

CHARLOTTE. I had begun to bicycle, but I rather think the enjoyment gone.

SHAW. *(crossing toward her)* Nonsense. After a single spill?

CHARLOTTE. We nearly collided.

SHAW. *(sitting on the arm of the sofa)* And look where it led me: alone with a charming and beautiful semi-clad woman. I consider it the most enjoyable bicycle excursion ever taken.

CHARLOTTE. Perhaps because your leg has never struck the pedal.

(SHAW stands and walks around her over the following, ending with a pose down left.)

SHAW. You're wrong. I have taken many a tumble on my bicycle. My head has hit trees, and my face boulders. I have flown into ravines, smashed into carriages. I call that living. I would gladly strike my entire body against the pedal to be in your shoes and spend an afternoon in conversation with the greatest mind in all England.

CHARLOTTE. And who would that be?

SHAW. Sidney Webb. The man with no vinegar. *(sitting in the desk chair beside her)* A staggeringly brilliant man. The ablest man in England. Quite the wisest thing I ever did was to force my friendship on him and to keep it.

CHARLOTTE. I thought you would say yourself.

SHAW. I would never call myself the greatest mind in all England. I would wait politely for you to say it. – And I'm certain you will, someday. All women do.

CHARLOTTE. Do they now?

SHAW. Actresses, mostly. Florence Farr, Janet Achurch, Ellen Terry.

CHARLOTTE. *The* Ellen Terry?

(SHAW crosses to his desk and waves the letter at CHARLOTTE.)

SHAW. Oh yes. She writes to me daily.

CHARLOTTE. And you?

SHAW. Well, one must respond.

    (**SHAW** *puts the letter back on the desk.*)

CHARLOTTE. Naturally.

SHAW. You say that as though I were at fault! Up to the time that I was twenty-nine, actually twenty-nine, I was too shabby for any woman to tolerate me. I stalked about in a green coat, cuffs trimmed with the scissors, terrible boots and so on. Then I got a job to do and bought a suit of clothes with the proceeds. Do you like it?

    (**SHAW** *turns around to display his outfit.*)

CHARLOTTE. I never saw anything like it.

SHAW. It's a Jaeger. All wool. Designed to allow the skin to breathe and to assist in the sweating out of bodily toxins.

CHARLOTTE. So you reserve the vegetables for the inside and the animals for the outside.

SHAW. *(crossing down right)* And it has worked miracles. The instant I donned these vestments a lady immediately invited me to tea, threw her arms around me, and said she adored me.

CHARLOTTE. And how did you respond?

SHAW. I permitted her to adore. *(crossing down left)* Since that time, whenever I have been left alone in a room with a female, she has invariably thrown her arms around me and declared she adored me. It is fate. *(sitting in the desk chair beside her)* Therefore beware. If you allow yourself to be left alone with me for a single moment, you will certainly throw your arms round me and declare you adore me; and I am not prepared to guarantee that my usual melancholy forbearance will be available in your case.

CHARLOTTE. Thank you. My injury, no doubt, prohibits the scene you have described.

SHAW. *(leaning back, luxuriously)* You can't think what delightful agony it is to be in love with me: my genius for hurting women is extraordinary; and I always do it with the best intentions. My latest unintended conquest is an artist with whom Mrs. Webb has lumbered me. Bertha Newcombe is her name. She is painting my portrait.

CHARLOTTE. How is Mrs. Webb involved?

SHAW. She introduced Miss Newcombe to me, hoping I would fall under the spell of an intelligent woman with socialist tendencies and an artistic bent. *(leaning forward)* Apparently Mrs. Webb has an amusing notion that the best cure for freedom is slavery.

CHARLOTTE. Perhaps she would like to see you happy.

SHAW. *(standing)* Or perhaps she resents the liberty and happiness of my bachelorhood, and strives unmercifully to indenture me to a spouse.

CHARLOTTE. I doubt Mrs. Webb could be as devious as that.

*(**SHAW** crosses down right.)*

SHAW. Tell me. Do you find yourself lately sent down with Graham Wallas to an absurd degree?

CHARLOTTE. Well, yes, but…do you mean to say – !?

SHAW. *(Laughing. Turning to her.)* Anagnoresis! Worthy of the Ancient Greeks.

CHARLOTTE. What makes you think Mrs. Webb is trying to create a match between Mr. Wallas and myself?

SHAW. *(crossing to the sofa)* Because that is what she does. The moment Beatrice mentioned your coming, she was careful also to mention Wallas and to downplay your attractiveness to me.

CHARLOTTE. Did she now.

SHAW. And traditionally that is an indicator of the most deceitful machinations on her part.

CHARLOTTE. Then I am exceedingly glad Mr. Wallas will not be attending.

SHAW. Wallas not attending!

CHARLOTTE. He telegraphed this morning to say he had business in London.

SHAW. *(crossing up left)* This is appalling! No Wallas?! From whom shall I steal you now? The glory of the hunt will be denied me.

CHARLOTTE. Don't speak to me of the glorious hunt, Mr. Shaw, you're plowing the wrong furrow. I have no intention of ever marrying.

SHAW. *(leaning against the mantel)* I assure you, my intentions are in no way honorable.

CHARLOTTE. I don't know if I can quite take assurance from that.

(SHAW crosses to the up left corner of the sofa.)

SHAW. I would have expected a more conventional view of marriage from you.

CHARLOTTE. Based upon what? My manners? My income? You're not the only Irish nonconformist, Mr. Shaw.

SHAW. *(sitting in the desk chair)* You blame Ireland for your radical views?

CHARLOTTE. I blame my mother. It was her one regret on the day she died.

SHAW. She despised being married?

CHARLOTTE. She despised my *not* being married. And since I despised her, I have remained single.

SHAW. All children should follow your example.

CHARLOTTE. I almost wavered a few months ago. Axel Munthe. A French doctor of mesmerism.

SHAW. *(standing)* A French doctor of mesmerism??? Can such a monster truly stalk the earth? *(crossing down left)* It is dreadful enough to contemplate the existence of doctors, without having to contend with the horror of a degree in mesmerism! …The mind reels at the unwelcome addition of France to the mixture!

CHARLOTTE. If he had ever proposed, I might have accepted.

SHAW. Whatever for?

CHARLOTTE. I felt alone.

SHAW. *(crossing to down right)* You sound like Webb. It would take more than mere isolation to force me into marriage. It would take immobility! Broken bones! All the powers of hell! And even then, I would consider it the greatest defeat of my existence. Wedlock is a heavy chain for a man to rivet upon himself.

CHARLOTTE. The married man is not the only one in chains, Mr. Shaw. The woman feels the restraint just as painfully as he.

SHAW. Yes, but the woman is born with the chain on: to her, wedlock only means riveting the other end of it upon a man. Abolish wedlock, and the man is free; but the woman is left to bear the whole weight of her servitude alone.

CHARLOTTE. But that sounds as if you favor marriage for a woman.

SHAW. *(crossing above the sofa to up left)* What choice does a woman have, when she may not effect any social change through the avenues available to a man? She may not vote, or hold public office, or acquire a university degree. It is likely she will not find employment beyond that of a clark or a barmaid.

CHARLOTTE. And yet she enjoys greater rights before the law on her own than as a wife. If an unmarried woman is struck by a man, the man is reviled as the basest form of brute and hauled before a magistrate; but if a husband strikes his wife, her demands for justice are ignored by the courts because it is a matter for the family.

*(A beat as **SHAW** enjoys the intellectual energy of their conversation. He speaks more intimately as he sits beside her.)*

SHAW. You and I are in complete agreement on this matter; England needs to address the contradictions. The only way for a woman to improve her lot is to be born pretty enough or rich enough to marry well.

CHARLOTTE. And which of these am I?

SHAW. Both, I assure you.

CHARLOTTE. You *are* the greatest mind in all England.

SHAW. That took longer than expected. – If you intend to marry, marry well and marry as an equal. If you do not intend to marry, find employment; better society. That is the course I have chosen to navigate.

CHARLOTTE. Then I shall be your first mate.

SHAW. Well done.

> *(They shake hands. He does not release it.)*

How are you feeling?

CHARLOTTE. Better. Thank you.

> *(CHARLOTTE discreetly covers her leg again. SHAW stands.)*

SHAW. I was going to telegraph a madman before our little dustup. Would you care to accompany me?

CHARLOTTE. On bicycle?

SHAW. It would do you good to hop back on it immediately.

CHARLOTTE. ...Yes. Thank you. I would love to.

> *(SHAW offers a hand of assistance. CHARLOTTE takes it as she stands. They share another moment.)*

SHAW. Beatrice was completely wrong about you. Your eyes are not gray, they're green.

CHARLOTTE. You are a charmer, aren't you, Mr. Shaw?

SHAW. *(retrieving his cap from the hook)* Ach, such formality will never do! I shall call you Charlotte and you shall call me Shaw.

CHARLOTTE. Just Shaw? I couldn't possibly.

SHAW. Why not?

CHARLOTTE. Shaw? Whenever I call you, it will sound like I'm scoffing.

SHAW. How's GBS?

CHARLOTTE. *(moving closer to SHAW)* What does the G stand for?

SHAW. No, no. Nobody calls me George. I am Bernard in town and Sonny at home.

CHARLOTTE. Bernie, then.

SHAW. *(poorly hiding his disgust)* …Bernie it is.

*(**SHAW** offers his arm to **CHARLOTTE** as they head toward the french window. **WEBB** and **BEATRICE** enter from the house with a small parcel.)*

WEBB. We've secured a beefsteak.

CHARLOTTE. A beefsteak? Whatever for?

SHAW. Intellect the caliber of mine can not derive nutriment from cow!

*(**SHAW** dramatically dons his cap. Scene change music begins as **SHAW** and **CHARLOTTE** exit. The lights fade.)*

Scene 2

(The same room, two weeks later. SHAW is seated at his desk, typing a love letter to Ellen Terry. But his focus is on CHARLOTTE, who is seated on the sofa, reading one of SHAW's plays. She slams the script shut and audibly expresses disgust. SHAW turns to her.)

CHARLOTTE. *The Philanderer.*

SHAW. You're not enjoying it?

CHARLOTTE. I'd rather there were less philandering in it.

SHAW. *(removing the letter from the typewriter)* As would I, but my journalistic background compels me to expose the truth about the many women who love and hate me so passionately.

CHARLOTTE. Rubbish.

SHAW. *(signing the letter)* It *is* rubbish. I agree with you.

CHARLOTTE. You don't agree with me, but you say so to be amusingly shocking.

SHAW. *(giving her his full attention)* Enough about me. Let's talk about my play.

CHARLOTTE. Let's not. I much prefer the new one.

SHAW. *The Devil's Disciple?*

CHARLOTTE. *(standing)* Or any of the others. They have a seriousness of purpose that *The Philanderer* lacks. But really...I've said enough.

(CHARLOTTE crosses away from him, up left, holding the script.)

SHAW. There's more? Let's have it out.

CHARLOTTE. *(turning to him)* ...Only because you asked, mind, this is not the sort of thing I'd tell just anyone.

SHAW. Naturally. Like most people, you reserve your strongest insults for friends.

CHARLOTTE. *(crossing to him)* It's not an insult, it's a question. Why, when you are doing such important work with your speeches and essays, when you have made a career as a music and drama critic, why must you squander your energy as a disappointed dramatist?

(**SHAW** *stands, holding the letter, and crosses down left, away from* **CHARLOTTE**.)

SHAW. I am not disappointed. The curiosity and interest shown in my plays by managers have exceeded anything I had any right to expect.

CHARLOTTE. You've not had a single one of your plays produced beyond a copyright performance. You don't consider that unsuccessful?

SHAW. Of course not. *(crossing toward her, above the sofa)* In the present condition of the theater it is evident that a dramatist like Ibsen, who disregards the managers, and throws himself on the reading public, is taking the only course in which any serious advance is possible. So, like Ibsen, I have made up my mind to put my plays into print and trouble the theater no further with them. *(crossing to the other desk for an envelope)* And if you prefer, I will trouble *you* no further with them as well.

(**SHAW** *puts the letter in an envelope.* **CHARLOTTE** *crosses toward him.*)

CHARLOTTE. It is no trouble. I enjoy both your work and your company. I make no secret of it. They have been the highlight of the past two weeks.

SHAW. But you'd rather not read any more of *The Philanderer*.

CHARLOTTE. No.

(**CHARLOTTE** *hands* **SHAW** *his manuscript. He crosses to his desk with the manuscript and the sealed letter. He sits at the desk and returns to work.* **CHARLOTTE** *crosses up left of his desk, wanting his attention.*)

What are you working on now?

SHAW. *(turning to her)* I'm getting *The Devil's Disciple* ready for Richard Mansfield, an English actor/manager who has proven so *un*successful in his home country that

America has fallen in love with him. He believes the play might have an audience in New York. *(returning to work)* But editing the others for publication is taking more time than I thought.

CHARLOTTE. *(crossing toward the book case up left)* I couldn't write a paragraph, let alone a play or a book. Where do you find the energy?

SHAW. It springs from necessity, if I hope to have them published by the end of the year.

CHARLOTTE. *(turning to him)* You should hire a secretary.

SHAW. Who could possibly suffer my mercurial temper?

CHARLOTTE. *(crossing down left)* People will do anything for money – even work for Bernard Shaw.

SHAW. *(glancing over his shoulder at her)* What if I have no money to offer?

CHARLOTTE. Then you find someone with an emotional commitment.

SHAW. *(turning to her, fully engaged)* Emotional commitment is precisely the commitment I wish to avoid. The proximity of extreme emotions indicates that they are temporal and foolish.

CHARLOTTE. The proximity of extreme emotions?

SHAW. Love and hate being different expressions of the same basic feeling.

CHARLOTTE. That's not true.

SHAW. *(standing)* It is. I can show you. I live with it every day. **(SHAW** *crosses below the sofa.)* You may have heard me speak about all of my amours?

CHARLOTTE. You speak of little else.

SHAW. All of them save one have been married.

CHARLOTTE. …How very interesting.

SHAW. That is my modus operandi. I find a couple, wherein the husband is exceedingly busy and neglectful and the wife exceedingly pretty and frustrated, and I attach myself to them.

CHARLOTTE. In what way?

SHAW. I see them socially. I visit the wife when the husband is gone. I get invited to their homes in the country. And I flirt with the wife and ignore the husband with no danger of reprisal.

(**SHAW** *sits on the sofa, triumphantly.*)

CHARLOTTE. *(crossing toward him)* The husbands don't object?

SHAW. They are grateful. It saves them the bother of flirting with their wives themselves. Besides, they think me no danger, I'm good old Shaw.

(**SHAW** *pats the cushion beside him as an invitation to* **CHARLOTTE**. *She sits.*)

CHARLOTTE. What about the wives?

SHAW. We have great times together: playing the piano, conversing. I treat them as equals and they adore it. They are made to feel attractive again.

CHARLOTTE. And then they fall in love with you and you depart.

SHAW. *(standing)* I'm not there for love. *(crossing down right)* I'm there to provide a small amount of happiness; to do, for a short while, the job the husband should be doing in the first place.

(**SHAW** *sits at his desk again.*)

CHARLOTTE. What does this have to do with the proximity of love and hate?

SHAW. *(turning to her with impish pleasure)* You may notice that I currently reside in a similar situation to the one just described.

CHARLOTTE. *(too loud)* You and Mrs. Webb...!!???

(**SHAW** *hushes* **CHARLOTTE**. *He crosses down left quickly and looks off, to make sure he will not be overheard. He turns to* **CHARLOTTE**.*)*

SHAW. I don't flirt with Beatrice. She won't let me. In fact, she doesn't appear to like me in the least. *(crossing up left, showing off)* I'm not even human; I'm a sprite But you see, that's false. Her outward venom is a mask of her true feelings.

CHARLOTTE. Bernie, you are straining credulity today.

SHAW. *(crossing up left of the sofa)* Why do you think Beatrice is so eager to see me married? Because as a virile, unattached man I am a threat to her happy marriage.

CHARLOTTE. *(standing, moving down right)* You are the most self-centered man I have ever met.

SHAW. Beatrice did not marry for love. She married the man best suited to help her succeed as an advocate for socialism. *(moving below the sofa)* I am not saying her marriage isn't happy. If all marriages were as happy, England, and indeed the civilized world, would be a Fabian paradise. But she is a passionate woman with a dispassionate mate, and is afraid she may find passion elsewhere. The fact that she hates me proves that she loves me.

CHARLOTTE. *(crossing to down left)* What woman pines for a celibate Don Juan?

SHAW. In my experience: All of them. *(crossing to* CHARLOTTE*)* My effect on Beatrice is no different from Bertha Newcombe, or any of the others. Mind what she does next time we are all together.

CHARLOTTE. Not every woman finds you irresistible.

SHAW. *(crossing to his desk)* Now you're being silly.

CHARLOTTE. *(Stopping him. Stepping toward the center.)* I don't find you irresistible.

SHAW. *(moving to her)* That's because there is nothing to resist; we are always together. And you won't leave me, because you like me. You like me too much to fall in love with me. Should you ever feel the urge to throttle me, be careful; for then you'll be in love.

CHARLOTTE. You are insufferable.

(**CHARLOTTE** *moves up left, as* **SHAW** *heads toward his desk.*)

SHAW. Mind Beatrice.

(**WEBB** *and* **BEATRICE** *enter from down left.* **WEBB** *struggles with a tall, thin crate.*)

WEBB. Just delivered.

SHAW. Let me help you with that.

(**SHAW** *gives directional gestures, but does not touch the crate. Eventually, the crate is deposited on the sofa.* **CHARLOTTE** *and* **BEATRICE** *are stage left, with* **CHARLOTTE** *being furthest left.* **SHAW** *and* **WEBB** *are stage right.*)

CHARLOTTE. What is it?

BEATRICE. We can guess.

CHARLOTTE. Who is it from?

BEATRICE. Bertha Newcombe for Shaw.

WEBB. *(grabbing his hand)* Blast!

(**BEATRICE** *crosses to* **WEBB** *and begins to baby his hand.*)

BEATRICE. Oh, dear boy, did you hurt yourself? Let me see.

WEBB. Just a splinter.

SHAW. I'll get a knife.

(**SHAW** *exits down right, signaling* **CHARLOTTE** *to watch* **BEATRICE**. **BEATRICE** *releases* **WEBB**'s *hand and crosses to* **CHARLOTTE**.)

BEATRICE. There you go. Shaw will deal with it.

(**BEATRICE** *focusses on* **CHARLOTTE** *and the crate.* **WEBB** *struggles to remove the splinter alone.*)

We are guessing this is the painting. Shaw was posing for months.

WEBB. Devilishly painful.

BEATRICE. Yes, Bertha's not very good company, I'm afraid.

(SHAW meets CHARLOTTE up center before they head toward the up right exit. BEATRICE counters left. WEBB struggles to get the crate off stage down right. BEATRICE stops them all.)

BEATRICE. Actually, Charlotte, Sidney and I had hoped to speak with you upon a matter of business.

(This is news to WEBB, as he struggles with the crate.)

…I hope we're not spoiling your plans.

CHARLOTTE. – I can stay behind.

WEBB. *(Genuinely pleased. Placing the crate down right.)* Capital.

CHARLOTTE. Any problem with that, Bernie?

SHAW. Why all of a sudden take *my* feelings into account?

CHARLOTTE. *(smiling)* Just go.

SHAW. With all speed, milady.

(SHAW dons his cap and exits up right. CHARLOTTE is up center, the apex of a Fabian triangle.)

BEATRICE. You and Shaw seem to have made a fast friendship. You're never out of each other's company.

CHARLOTTE. Have I monopolized his time?

WEBB. Beatrice meant nothing unkind. We are glad to see it; it makes the two of you happy, and it allows Beatrice and me the tender solitude we prefer when writing about economic disparity.

BEATRICE. You are a welcome addition to the Bo family.

WEBB. The Bo family. That's what Beatrice calls her closest friends.

CHARLOTTE. I'm flattered.

(WEBB gestures for CHARLOTTE to sit on the sofa. She does. BEATRICE sits beside her to the right.)

BEATRICE. Yes, if you want to learn anything about anything, Shaw is the man to teach you.

CHARLOTTE. I have certainly learned a lot this morning.

(WEBB takes the chair from his desk and sits on the other side of CHARLOTTE.)

WEBB. I am glad to hear it. Beatrice and I are firm believers in the value of education. Not the type found in traditional schools. But a new kind, based upon practical circumstances.

BEATRICE. This is why we founded the London School of Economics. Unfortunately, the school is in such perilous financial shape, we may be forced to decline an invitation to America.

CHARLOTTE. Oh no, you must go.

WEBB. And I had planned to stand for London County Council, but Beatrice feels that we really can't ignore the school until a benefactor steps forward to provide it with – long-term solvency.

CHARLOTTE. And this is where I come in.

WEBB. Well...

BEATRICE. We've secured a building in Adelphi Terrace with more room than we require, in the hope that we will soon expand.

CHARLOTTE. Bernie keeps an office there, doesn't he?

WEBB. That's where he spends most of his time, when he's not at home or the theater.

CHARLOTTE. Very interesting. How many vacant rooms does the school still have? Could any of them operate as a flat?

BEATRICE. The top floor could be converted.

CHARLOTTE. I am looking for a flat in London after the Summer. My money is better spent on your school than the enrichment of a landlord. How does three hundred pounds per annum sound?

WEBB. We couldn't possibly ask that much.

(**BEATRICE** *shoots him a look. He explains to her.*)

The entire building rents at four hundred.

CHARLOTTE. That is immaterial. The school needs the money, and so you shall have it.

WEBB. Most generous, Charlotte.

BEATRICE. If there's anything we can do to repay you –

CHARLOTTE. *(standing)* Actually…there is something I would like –

WEBB. Certainly.

> (**CHARLOTTE** *crosses down right.*)

CHARLOTTE. – in exchange for my assistance.

WEBB. *(standing)* – in exchange, certainly. What is it?

CHARLOTTE. …Bernie.

WEBB. …What!

CHARLOTTE. I want Bernie.

> *(a beat)*

WEBB. Am I hearing you correctly, Miss Payne-Townshend? You expect us to hand Shaw over to you bodily in exchange for three hundred pounds?

CHARLOTTE. You misunderstand.

WEBB. Thank God for that!

CHARLOTTE. I want you to arrange for him to fall in love with me.

WEBB. What???

CHARLOTTE. *(crossing right of the sofa)* With a little assistance from you, I could manage the rest. No man can resist a woman once she has set her sights upon him, unless thwarted by another woman.

WEBB. What sort of a notion is that?!

CHARLOTTE. Your wife knows perfectly well what I am talking about.

WEBB. I am confident she does not.

BEATRICE. What Sidney means, Charlotte, is that Shaw may prove difficult to deliver.

WEBB. To deliver??? Beatrice! You speak of him as though he were a piano! Let me assure you, ladies, with utmost emphasis: Bernard Shaw is *not* a piano. *(crossing down left)* And neither am I a piano! We are men. We are not to be delivered to women in exchange for sterling. We are not to be played upon for an evening's entertainment. We are not to be tuned before the arrival of important guests. No man is a piano!

BEATRICE. This is really a conversation for the women, Sidney.

WEBB. I think a man's opinion is just the thing this subject requires.

BEATRICE. *(crossing to him)* Dear boy, why don't you wait in the other room?

WEBB. *(crossing away, down right)* Neither am I a child, Beatrice. I refuse –

BEATRICE. There's a plate of chocolate on the sideboard.

WEBB. No! My wrath will not be appeased by chocolate: I am a man!

BEATRICE. It's Swiss.

WEBB. Is it? *(beat)* Yes, all right.

*(***WEBB*** makes the long cross to down left before announcing:)*

But I'm still very upset.

*(***WEBB*** exits down left. A beat as the women regard each other with polite smiles. ***CHARLOTTE*** sits on the sofa. ***BEATRICE*** fetches a tray of tea and sits beside ***CHARLOTTE***. ***BEATRICE*** pours them both tea over the following.)*

BEATRICE. I must say, I have seriously misjudged you. When first we met you seemed little more than a pleasant, well-dressed, well-intentioned woman with a large income. Now you turn out to be an "original."

CHARLOTTE. I apologize for my bluntness, Mrs. Webb.

BEATRICE. Not at all. I find it refreshing.

CHARLOTTE. I feel that you and I are alike in many respects. We both prefer the company of men to the company of other women.

BEATRICE. On the contrary, I have devoted my entire life to fighting for women's rights.

CHARLOTTE. In the abstract, yes. But on a personal level, we tend to see other women as rivals.

BEATRICE. Why should I see any woman as my rival? Rival for what? I would hope you have never viewed me as a rival for anything. I know I have never seen you as such.

CHARLOTTE. …Perhaps the observation was inapt.

(Beat. They sip.)

BEATRICE. You know Shaw will never marry.

CHARLOTTE. Then why have you endeavored so assiduously to engage him to Miss Newcombe?

*(***BEATRICE*** is caught.)*

If you want me to finance your school, you must put a stop to all plotting in Bernie's romantic affairs.

BEATRICE. Even if I did, I cannot promise he will marry you.

CHARLOTTE. I don't want marriage. My mother dominated and destroyed her marriage, then tried to condemn me to the same fate. I cursed my lot as a woman until I read Bernie's book. – I want exclusivity.

BEATRICE. You wish to be his mistress?

CHARLOTTE. *(standing, crossing down left)* Sex? God, no. I can think of nothing more repulsive than the matter-of-fact side of marriage.

BEATRICE. Oh, I don't know…

CHARLOTTE. *(crossing up left)* But I resent the enforced celibacy that society requires of me. I'd rather be celibate on my own terms, than those of male prelates.

BEATRICE. Shaw has no interest in sex either.

CHARLOTTE. Thank you, I am aware of it. Bernie and I are on very confidential terms and have explained our relative positions. *(crossing up left of the sofa)* – I require an ally. I cannot simultaneously engage Bernie and stave off every woman with a claim on his affection.

BEATRICE. The list is long.

CHARLOTTE. *(sitting beside* ***BEATRICE*** *again)* I suspect most are simply flirtations. There are only two women who concern me. The first is Bertha Newcombe. I should like you to take my part and forsake her.

BEATRICE. What about Ellen Terry? He'll never give off writing to her.

CHARLOTTE. I will deal with the second woman once Miss Newcombe is no longer an issue.

BEATRICE. How will you engage him?

CHARLOTTE. I shall become indispensable.

BEATRICE. All of Shaw's lovers have tried to be rid of their competitors. What makes you think you will fare differently?

CHARLOTTE. I'm Irish.

BEATRICE. The minute you bore him, he will turn away.

CHARLOTTE. You have known him longer than I. What do you suggest?

BEATRICE. *(feigning innocence)* I haven't the foggiest.

(BEATRICE catches CHARLOTTE's eye and acquiesces.)

– But he likes to teach.

CHARLOTTE. – Tell me I have an ally, and you shall have a school.

(SHAW enters from down left.)

BEATRICE. You have an ally.

SHAW. What secret cabal is this?

CHARLOTTE. Is your masculinity threatened? Yes, Bernie, the women are now in league.

(BEATRICE and CHARLOTTE laugh like fellow conspirators. SHAW hangs his hat on the hook and crosses toward his desk, stopping to speak to BEATRICE. BEATRICE grabs CHARLOTTE's hand for strength.)

SHAW. The entire household grows cryptic. Your husband instructed me to tell you that he has eaten all the chocolate.

BEATRICE. Then I had better apologize.

(BEATRICE exits down left.)

SHAW. What do you think, was I right?

CHARLOTTE. You're always right. About what?

SHAW. About Beatrice.

CHARLOTTE. *(standing)* Didn't notice a thing.

    *(**SHAW** sits at his desk and begins to work.)*

    Did you post your letter to Miss Terry?

SHAW. With alacrity.

CHARLOTTE. *(crossing to the bookcase up left)* What do you say to her in your letters?

SHAW. Desperate and romantic protestations, artfully concocted to inflame her passion and jealousy. I never disappoint.

CHARLOTTE. Do you tell her about me?

SHAW. Naturally, if I wish to arouse her jealousy. I told her that you positively doted upon *The Quintessence of Ibsenism.* She responded that if you did not dote on the quintessence of *me*, you'd better marry my book.

CHARLOTTE. *(crossing above the sofa)* Very interesting. Is she as beautiful in real life as she appears on the stage?

SHAW. I don't know. I've never met her.

CHARLOTTE. But you write to her every day.

SHAW. Oh yes. We've been making wild, passionate love to each other through the Royal Mail for many years now. But she has never set eyes on me.

CHARLOTTE. You have no desire to see the woman in person?

SHAW. I see her on the stage whenever I can.

CHARLOTTE. *(crossing above his desk)* But to converse, to gaze into each other's eyes…

SHAW. And kill romance?

CHARLOTTE. *(crossing down right)* You would satisfy the romance.

SHAW. And in doing so kill it.

    *(**CHARLOTTE** crosses down left. **SHAW** stands.)*

Romance is longing, it is unrelenting torture, and therefore the most pleasurable experience known to man.

(SHAW crosses to center, below the sofa.)

Once romance is satisfied it ceases to be romance. It becomes a bad habit and numbingly dull. But again, you must keep in mind that all romantic feelings in the relationship reside entirely within her breast. I am merely the verbally effusive object of her adulation.

CHARLOTTE. What sorts of things do you write to her?

SHAW. It will please you to know that I have written dozens of love letters by using up all the things I've said to you these past two weeks.

CHARLOTTE. *(moving toward him)* And that would please me? That you're sharing with other women the romantic nothings you've said to me? You don't think I should take offense at this?

SHAW. Of course not. Written or spoken, a romantic nothing is still, in the end, a nothing. *(picking up the knife)* But you get yours fresh from the butcher. And witness the miracle of their creation, as I filet them before your very eyes. No rank, decaying nostrums for you.

(Sitting at the desk, loading the typewriter.)

But, if you'd rather be on the other end, I can leave you notes filled with nonsense I've cribbed from conversations with Bertha.

(SHAW types quickly. He removes the page and reads it over the following.)

They're not half as wistful as the ones you've inspired, which are proving tremendously effective in town.

(He offers her the page. She doesn't take it, crossing up left, and looking at the painting. He returns to work.)

CHARLOTTE. It must be a dreadful distraction from all of your important work: transcribing romantic nothings to actresses, posing for portraits.

SHAW. Bertha's paintings are not as bad as they look.

CHARLOTTE. Not the painting, your time and energy. Why squander the life force?

SHAW. *(turning to her)* You haven't reached the point where you begin to curtail my freedom, have you? *(standing)* Discussions such as these do not bode well. I have ended many a relationship upon such circumstances.

CHARLOTTE. *(crossing down left)* A relationship! What are you saying?

SHAW. *(crossing center, below the sofa)* You know exactly what I am saying: that only for Ellen Terry, Bertha Newcombe, Florence Farr, and Janet Achurch, I should be utterly lonely without you.

CHARLOTTE. *(turning to him)* Listen to yourself, past forty and still going on like that. You sound as though you were falling in love with me.

SHAW. Nonsense. I like you so much that falling in love with you would be superfluous. But I will not have my wings clipped.

(He returns to the desk. She advances to center.)

CHARLOTTE. You are free to strut your plumage. I merely observed that if you were to stop posing for portraits and writing to actresses, you would no longer require a secretary.

SHAW. *(working)* Undoubtedly you are correct. But I would never deny gainful employment to someone who seeks it. I'd be a fine socialist, then.

CHARLOTTE. But you can't afford to pay a wage. You'd be a fine employer, then.

SHAW. Either I will find someone to do it gratis, or I will find the money. It's all a matter of conscious effort; an application of the will.

CHARLOTTE. Why don't I become your secretary?

SHAW. *(turning to her)* You? – No. No, I don't think so.

CHARLOTTE. You've already told me that a woman must either get married or find work. Well, you know my feelings about marriage, so why not work for you?

SHAW. Our current arrangement is only good through the summer. Come Autumn I return to London.

CHARLOTTE. I plan to go to London also.

SHAW. For how long?

CHARLOTTE. I just negotiated a year's rent on a flat.

SHAW. Where?

CHARLOTTE. At the London School of Economics in Adelphi Terrace.

SHAW. *(standing)* I keep an office there!

CHARLOTTE. How very interesting! *(crossing down left)* ...I could guarantee you a year's work at least.

SHAW. *(moving to center, below the sofa)* I'm intrigued.

CHARLOTTE. I have other advantages too.

SHAW. Oh?

CHARLOTTE. *(turning to him)* I won't require a wage.

SHAW. That is a necessary advantage.

CHARLOTTE. *(crossing to him)* And we enjoy each other's company.

SHAW. Do we?

CHARLOTTE. At least you enjoy mine. – And you will have the pleasure of employing a relative of the man who first employed you.

SHAW. I must confess that is one of your chief attractions.

CHARLOTTE. Are we agreed?

SHAW. You make a strong case. ...Yes, I think we –

CHARLOTTE. *(interrupting, crossing down right)* No. No, it will never work. Forget I even mentioned it.

SHAW. What's the matter?

CHARLOTTE. I've led such a dreadfully useless, upper-class existence.

SHAW. *(moving to her)* It couldn't have been that upper-class, you are Irish.

CHARLOTTE. You won't think any less of me?

SHAW. Never, my dear green-eyed one.

(**CHARLOTTE** *crosses to down left. She faces away from him.*)

CHARLOTTE. I don't know how to type. How can I be your secretary when I don't know how to type?

SHAW. *(advancing to center)* Stuff and nonsense. Is that all? Typing is child's play. I can *teach* you.

CHARLOTTE. *(turning to him)* Could you? – I'm not a particularly good student.

SHAW. No matter, I am a particularly good teacher. A week under my tutelage and your fingers will fly across the keys.

CHARLOTTE. Then we are agreed.

SHAW. Take my hand and we can begin immediately.

(**SHAW** *extends a hand. She doesn't take it.*)

CHARLOTTE. Bernie, I'm to be your secretary, not your solicitor. Surely there is a less formal way to seal our agreement than a handshake.

SHAW. What did you have in mind?

CHARLOTTE. *(crossing to him)* I don't know. Perhaps…

(**CHARLOTTE** *kisses* **SHAW**. *The kiss is too long to be considered a peck, yet not long enough to be considered seriously romantic.*)

SHAW. Yes. I think this will work out quite well.

(*Scene change music begins as the lights fade.*)

Scene 3

*(Spot on **WEBB** down right. Lights come up slowly as he speaks, to reveal the same room as before. **CHARLOTTE** sits at **WEBB**'s desk, typing what he says.)*

WEBB. The community must necessarily aim, consciously or not, at its continuance as a community: its life transcends that of any of its members; and the interests of the individual unit must often clash with those of the whole.

*(**WEBB** opens a cigarette case.)*

CHARLOTTE. Oh. Sorry. The smoke.

WEBB. *(closing the cigarette case)* I'm the one who should apologize. It's bad business, I know, but I think better when my lungs are occupied.

CHARLOTTE. It will make you all the more respectable in America.

*(**WEBB** crosses center, below the sofa.)*

WEBB. Bo didn't tell you? We declined the invitation. She had qualms.

CHARLOTTE. Problems with the book?

WEBB. Oh no. It's at the publishers now. "Industrial Democracy" it's called. We hope it will be a modern *Wealth of Nations*. I honestly don't know what set Bo against the journey. Love for the native turf, I suppose.

CHARLOTTE. Love for something.

WEBB. And now that I've been elected to the London County Council, it is perhaps best I serve a term or two before we flit across the ocean. Which reminds me:

*(crossing to **CHARLOTTE**)*

Now that I'm the first Fabian to enter the political realm, I need you to convince Shaw to stand for something also.

*(**CHARLOTTE** stands.)*

There's an open vestry seat in Saint Pancras.

(**CHARLOTTE** *crosses to the other desk.*)

CHARLOTTE. You'll need to ask him when he returns.

(**BEATRICE** *enters from down left in traveling garb. She removes her hat.*)

BEATRICE. I'm back

WEBB. There's the partner of my life and work!

(**WEBB** *crosses to* **BEATRICE** *and helps her to remove her coat.*)

BEATRICE. Shaw's on his way. I passed him in the coach.

WEBB. Excellent. Then we may return to working in our proper pairings. I'm half a person without Bo.

(**WEBB** *moves center, above the sofa.* **BEATRICE** *hangs her coat and hat on the hook.* **CHARLOTTE** *and* **BEATRICE** *begin speaking with hidden significance, confusing* **WEBB.**)

CHARLOTTE. …So, Beatrice: How was London?

WEBB. Ah!

BEATRICE. …More difficult than I anticipated.

WEBB. Oh dear.

CHARLOTTE. …But was it successful?

WEBB. Yes?

BEATRICE. – I believe it was. Yes.

WEBB. I don't know that I'm quite following this conversation. Ordinarily, I would excuse myself, but we seem to be out of chocolate, so…

(**WEBB** *senses that his joke has fallen flat. He withers.*)

Right.

(**WEBB** *exits down right.* **CHARLOTTE** *turns to* **BEATRICE** *with anticipation.*)

BEATRICE. You need not concern yourself with Bertha Newcombe any longer.

(*They sit on the sofa.*)

CHARLOTTE. Tell me everything.

BEATRICE. Apparently there is a rumor flying through all London that you and Shaw are shortly to be married.

CHARLOTTE. Truly?

BEATRICE. Bertha wrote a letter, demanding an explanation from Shaw, who defended your honor by severing their relationship.

CHARLOTTE. *Very* interesting.

BEATRICE. I thought so.

CHARLOTTE. How did she take it?

BEATRICE. Not well. When I arrived, the poor woman was elated to see me, desperate for my assistance. I told her I had none to offer. I said: I should have welcomed her as Shaw's wife, but directly I saw that he meant nothing I backed out of the affair. She appealed to my friendship, but I had to be honest: I never considered her a personal friend of mine or Sidney's. I always regarded her as Shaw's friend.

CHARLOTTE. You told her that?

BEATRICE. The truth must always come as a bolt to be effective.

CHARLOTTE. It seems horribly cruel.

BEATRICE. There were tears, naturally. And I melted a little. I told her she was well out of it. As a friend and a colleague, as a critic and literary thinker, there are few men for whom I have so warm a liking; but in his relations with women he is vulgar, if not worse; it is a vulgarity that includes cruelty and springs from vanity. – Before I left, Miss Newcombe confessed that knowing the truth is more peaceful than being kept on the rack.

CHARLOTTE. Like the peace of death. Poor woman. *(crossing down right)* – Oh Beatrice, sending you to break another woman's heart, what have I become?

BEATRICE. You have done nothing shameful. Shaw had already broken with Miss Newcombe. Her interests needed to be sacrificed for the good of the community.

I feel no remorse for my part; I take pride in it. She suffered under an illusion and we led her to the truth. I have never in my life had an illusion dispelled without experiencing joy and gratitude.

CHARLOTTE. If true, you make my next task that much easier.

BEATRICE. I am always grateful when the scales fall from my eyes. When you speak to Miss Terry, I should hope you are as direct as I was with Miss Newcombe.

CHARLOTTE. *(turning to* **BEATRICE***)* I shall be direct. ... Beatrice –

BEATRICE. Is there something the matter?

CHARLOTTE. Beatrice…Miss Terry is not Shaw's other woman.

BEATRICE. No?

CHARLOTTE. – No. …It's you.

(*A beat.* **BEATRICE** *laughs.*)

BEATRICE. I have no interest in Shaw.

CHARLOTTE. But you do. I have seen it.

BEATRICE. Nonsense.

CHARLOTTE. It's true.

BEATRICE. Stop. You'll make me cross.

CHARLOTTE. Here he comes.

(**CHARLOTTE** *crosses to* **BEATRICE***, grabbing her hands and making her stand.*)

Mind what you do. Stand here and face him.

(**CHARLOTTE** *positions* **BEATRICE** *down center.* **SHAW** *enters from down left, looking windswept. He has obviously fallen from his bicycle, but refuses to admit it.*)

SHAW. Back from town and not a single spill! When once I have mastered that bicycle, it will no longer hold my interest.

(*Beat.* **SHAW** *relishes her discomfort.*)

BEATRICE. Sidney wanted to ask you something. Let me get him.

(**BEATRICE** *exits down right.*)

SHAW. You see?

CHARLOTTE. You should see your*self.*

(**SHAW** *gazes at himself in the mirror, ostensibly on the fourth wall down left.*)

SHAW. This will never do.

(**WEBB** *enters with* **BEATRICE**, *who is showing signs of emotional distress.*)

WEBB. There's the chap – .

SHAW. Not just yet. I'm unfit to be seen.

(**SHAW** *exits quickly past* **WEBB** *and* **BEATRICE** *down right.*)

WEBB. – Shaw!

(**WEBB** *exits rapidly after* **SHAW**. *A long pause, as the women tensely regard each other.*)

CHARLOTTE. You left.

BEATRICE. Sidney had a question –

CHARLOTTE. You couldn't face him.

BEATRICE. I could – I can – I – You must believe me: I love my husband.

CHARLOTTE. *(kindly) (crossing to her)* No one doubts it.

BEATRICE. I must beg you to leave this topic of conversation and never return to it.

CHARLOTTE. The truth should always come as a bolt, should it not?

BEATRICE. *(crossing up left)* This is *not* the truth. I don't love Shaw. – I hate Shaw.

CHARLOTTE. On the surface, yes, we all see that. But underneath –

(**BEATRICE** *scoffs.* **CHARLOTTE** *crosses to* **BEATRICE** *up left.*)

I know it's difficult.

(**BEATRICE** *counters up right.*)

CHARLOTTE. *(cont.)* I didn't believe it myself until Bernie showed me.

BEATRICE. *He* showed you? Then perhaps it is Shaw's affection for *me* that you witnessed, not mine for him.

CHARLOTTE. Would that please you?

BEATRICE. *(advancing on* **CHARLOTTE***)* What would please me, Miss Payne-Townshend, is never to speak with you again upon this, or any other subject. Damn your money! We do not want it. Such rude behavior is unforgivable.

(**CHARLOTTE** *suddenly grabs* **BEATRICE***'s hands as an affectionate warning. She speaks quickly.*)

CHARLOTTE. The money is yours whether I'm right or wrong. But if I'm wrong, why do my words affect you?

WEBB. *(off)* Shaw!

(**CHARLOTTE** *moves* **BEATRICE** *to center, below the sofa.*)

CHARLOTTE. Here they come. Stand here. Don't move to your husband when Bernie's present.

BEATRICE. What?

CHARLOTTE. He knows that you cling to Sidney as protection against your feelings. Stay right here.

(**CHARLOTTE** *backs away from* **BEATRICE** *to up left.* **SHAW** *enters from down right, followed by* **WEBB**. **SHAW** *heads to up left above the sofa.* **WEBB** *remains down right.*)

SHAW. I am not a politician!

WEBB. I can't be the only Fabian up there! I'll look like a glory-seeker!

SHAW. Only if you seek glory, a prospect I find dubious.

WEBB. *(a step toward* **BEATRICE***)* He deflects me with jokes. Talk to him.

(**BEATRICE** *looks at* **SHAW** *and begins to speak with a*

smile. But as she speaks, she unconsciously moves toward
WEBB *with a hand extended for him to hold.)*

BEATRICE. But Shaw, think of all the practical good you could –

*(*BEATRICE *realizes. She gasps and stops moving.* **SHAW** *moves farther down stage. He and the* **WEBB** *are parallel, with* **BEATRICE** *between them.)*

SHAW. There is not a morsel of practical good to be had from English politics until the party system is grabbed 'round the throat and has the life squeezed out of it.

WEBB. You hear that, Bo?

BEATRICE. *(trying not to move)* You don't like the party system?

SHAW. Until Parliament is able to seat "Shaw, party of one," I refuse it my patronage.

WEBB. I'm not urging Parliament upon you, merely a local vestry. St. Pancras, near Tottenham Court Road...

*(*SHAW *steps closer to* **WEBB** *with each "no."* **BEATRICE** *remains between them, in agony.)*

SHAW. No.

WEBB. Very poor area. It needs your help.

SHAW. No!

WEBB. It's a vestry. Simply concerned individuals. No parties.

SHAW. ...Very well.

*(*SHAW *moves away, down left.)*

WEBB. Capital! Bo, give us a hug.

*(*WEBB *stands with his arms open, but* **BEATRICE** *does nothing.)*

What's the matter? You're always keen for a hug when Shaw's around.

*(*BEATRICE *is shocked at* **WEBB**'s *observation. She breaks down.)*

BEATRICE. Oh, Sidney, take me away from here. Please, I want to go to America.

WEBB. We just turned down the invitation.

BEATRICE. *(clinging to* **WEBB***)* I don't care. I must leave this place. I need to travel for a long, long time. America, Australia, around the world!

SHAW. Is everything all right?

WEBB. Yes, we're – yes. No problem.

BEATRICE. Please, Sidney.

WEBB. Yes, of course, Bo. We'll go. Whatever you want.

*(***BEATRICE*** hugs him tightly again.)*

BEATRICE. Thank you. I do love you, my dear boy.

WEBB. Well, of course, and I love you.

(He starts to usher her off down right.)

BEATRICE. You do believe me, don't you Sidney?

WEBB. What a silly question! Come along…

*(And they are gone. ***SHAW*** crosses down right pensively. He turns to ***CHARLOTTE***.)*

SHAW. I'd be a poor detective if I didn't see your fingerprints all over that.

CHARLOTTE. A strange accusation from "The Snake in the Grass."

SHAW. *(crossing center, above the sofa)* I gave you that information in confidence.

CHARLOTTE. *(crossing to him)* I needed to lead her to the truth.

SHAW. So you're a Fabian now, are you?

(He turns away from her.)

CHARLOTTE. You don't think me capable.

SHAW. *(turning on her)* Plotting behind my back? That's the woman of yesterday. It's not the woman you could become.

CHARLOTTE. *(crossing down left)* What choice do women have, but to make clandestine plots?

SHAW. They have all the choice in the world, through willed evolution, to become anything they wish.

CHARLOTTE. Men won't allow it.

SHAW. Of course they will, once they realize the increased strength and emotional power they would achieve by sharing the stage with women.

CHARLOTTE. Then why don't you increase your strength and emotional power by sharing the stage with a woman?

SHAW. For the same reason that you do not with a man. *(crossing right of the sofa)* Besides, I have yet to find the woman who is my intellectual peer.

CHARLOTTE. *(crossing center, below the sofa)* I should pity my sex if we harbored the equal of you.

SHAW. *(crossing to her)* Is equality all you're after? You're aiming too low. A woman's natural power is far stronger than anything male-created society can bestow. *(crossing away from her down right)* Why are women so eager to forsake such an important, natural, and eternal purpose as motherhood for the transient trivialities of male-dominated society?

CHARLOTTE. Because men have reduced the social importance of maternity.

SHAW. *(crossing down left)* Why do the women believe them? Have men ever been right about anything?

CHARLOTTE. *(advancing on him)* Women may have the power to create life, but male society dictates how and when and where that power may be utilized. It is the man who calls his wife to bed as the mood strikes him, and she is compelled to obey whether she likes it or not.

SHAW. *(returning to his desk, but not sitting)* You obviously have little knowledge of the marital balance of power.

CHARLOTTE. I tread the knife's edge of sexual etiquette more frequently than you, Bernie. A woman may not express desire for a man for fear of dishonor, and she may not express displeasure for fear of abuse.

SHAW. There will come a day when women will have all of the equal social benefits of a man: they will vote, they will be doctors and solicitors and industrialists. *(crossing down right)* They will be spared the burden of matrimony and children, but they will be free to marry and conceive if that is their choice. *(crossing to* **CHARLOTTE** *down left)* There will come a time when women will be free to produce offspring without any assistance from men. On that day woman finally will be accepted as man's equal.

(A beat. **SHAW** *returns to his desk and sits.)*

CHARLOTTE. Conception without sex? Sex without conception? I can't imagine which is worse. What would be the point of either?

SHAW. *(working)* Pleasure, of course. And there's no worse torture than that.

(A pause. **CHARLOTTE** *crosses above the sofa, center.)*

CHARLOTTE. Is it pleasurable?

SHAW. Hm?

CHARLOTTE. Sex.

*(***SHAW*** *stops working and turns to her.)*

SHAW. Is sex pleasurable?

CHARLOTTE. *(crossing left of the sofa)* If you don't know, I und –

SHAW. I do know.

CHARLOTTE. Oh.

SHAW. ...Yes. It is pleasurable. – If I remember correctly.

CHARLOTTE. ...Who was she?

SHAW. A friend.

CHARLOTTE. Ah.

SHAW. Of my mother's.

CHARLOTTE. Oh. ...how did it make you feel?

SHAW. Triumphant. The glow was all-encompassing. *(standing)* I remember thinking that it must have been in a similar moment that Nietzche conceived the idea of the Superman. I am quite certain that the experience helped me as a writer and as a man, in fact I don't think I became a man until that night.

CHARLOTTE. You make it sound so lovely.

SHAW. It was, at first; but I soon found that my desire enslaved me. The woman used my lust like a weapon against me. *(crossing down right)* It put me into someone else's power, something that will never happen again. Having sex may have made me a man, but rejecting it made me Shaw.

CHARLOTTE. *(crossing down left)* It was separate from love?

SHAW. Very separate. It was physical, animal.

CHARLOTTE. ...Would you, perhaps, grant me the pleasure...of...granting me this pleasure?

SHAW. ...You want me – rather us – to...?

CHARLOTTE. I'm curious.

SHAW. Even so –

CHARLOTTE. And I'm tired of remaining celibate because men would have it so. ...I am forty years old and have no intention of marrying. I should like to become a woman.

(Pause. She crosses down center.)

CHARLOTTE. You are my best friend, Bernie; the only man I could ask to do this without fear of reprisal or misunderstanding.

SHAW. *(crossing toward her)* Yes, but think about what you are asking, my dear green-eyed one, and where it could lead. You will be unleashing emotions for which you are not prepared. From the moment that you can't do without me you're lost, like Bertha. Don't fall in love: be your own, not mine or anyone else's.

CHARLOTTE. *(moving closer to him)* How could I fall in love? It's purely a physical act, is it not? Like riding a bicycle.

SHAW. But once we return to London, we may fall off.

CHARLOTTE. I call that living.

*(***SHAW*** smiles. ***CHARLOTTE*** pulls away.)*

I hope no one will consider us a couple.

SHAW. Pay them no heed. If we want one another we shall find it out. *(taking her hands)* All I know is that you made the summer very happy, and that I shall always be fond of you for that. About the future I do not concern myself.

CHARLOTTE. Nor I.

*(***CHARLOTTE*** kisses ***SHAW***.)*

SHAW. My dearest.

*(***CHARLOTTE*** smiles and starts to exit provocatively down right. Music begins low.)*

Right now???

*(***CHARLOTTE*** nods, beckons him with the movement of a finger. Music increases. The lights fade and the act curtain descends as they exit down right.)*

ACT TWO

Scene 1

(The lights come up to reveal the same room in Stratford a year later. The portrait is gone. **CHARLOTTE** *types at the stage right desk, while* **SHAW** *lounges on the sofa, silently reading galley proofs of his book.* **SHAW** *suddenly laughs.* **CHARLOTTE** *stops typing.)*

SHAW. *Mrs. Warren.* It makes my blood run cold. It's much my best play, but I can hardly bear the most appalling bits of it. Ah, when I wrote this I had some nerve. And yet it's only three or four years ago – five at most.

*(***SHAW*** goes back to reading. Typing resumes. When* **CHARLOTTE** *completes the page, she tears it roughly from the typewriter and slams it on the stack of freshly typed pages beside her. No reaction from* **SHAW**. **CHARLOTTE** *inserts another sheet of paper into the typewriter and sighs loudly.)*

What's wrong?

CHARLOTTE. Nothing.

SHAW. Good. Then I'll return to the galleys. The publisher wants them back by tomorrow and I'm still in the Unpleasant volume. Will the preface be typed?

CHARLOTTE. Yes.

SHAW. We publish next month, you know.

CHARLOTTE. It is on the calendar.

SHAW. I'll be laboring at the preface to the second volume tonight. Both prefaces will be of the most flashing brilliancy.

(**CHARLOTTE** *sighs.* **SHAW** *goes back to reading.*
CHARLOTTE *sighs louder.*)

CHARLOTTE. You don't hear me sighing?

SHAW. I do. I thought you had developed whooping cough.

CHARLOTTE. Not funny.

SHAW. I apologize for the error. And for not instantly dropping my work like flaming rubbish and rushing to your comfort upon the sigh's first utterance. But since you had already informed me that nothing was wrong, I assumed it to be a sigh of love; a female sound I hear much too frequently, but one that I ignore less frequently than I should.

CHARLOTTE. Well, there is something wrong.

SHAW. And you expected to convey this to me through outright denials and salient exhalations? I have no magic powers, unlike your French doctor of mesmerism.

CHARLOTTE. If that's the way you're going to be, I shan't tell you.

SHAW. And deny me displeasure? You wouldn't dare. Of course you'll tell me, you're merely waiting for a more opportune moment to upset me.

(**CHARLOTTE** *returns to typing.* **SHAW** *sits up.*)

Come, Charlotte. Let's out with it.

(**CHARLOTTE** *stops typing.*)

CHARLOTTE. I went down to London yesterday to surprise you.

SHAW. *(standing)* Where were you? You might have given me lunch.

CHARLOTTE. I heard you speak in High Street.

SHAW. Yes?

CHARLOTTE. There it is.

SHAW. *(sitting again)* Ah, you didn't like what you heard. Well, you can scarcely blame me.

CHARLOTTE. So it's my fault, is it?

SHAW. I warned you to stay away.

CHARLOTTE. I refuse to shoulder the blame for your duplicity.

SHAW. Duplicity! When?

CHARLOTTE. *(standing)* In private you pretend to care for me, but in public you insult me.

SHAW. *(standing)* When did I insult you? I would never insult any woman in public. I never even mentioned your name yesterday.

CHARLOTTE. *(crossing down right)* You didn't need to; I understood what you were saying: "Destroy the wealthy! Burn their homes!" Is this what you mean by socialism?

(SHAW grabs a volume from the bookcase up left.)

SHAW. If you need a definition of socialism, I suggest you read Beatrice and Sidney's book, like the rest of the educated people in England.

(He crosses back to CHARLOTTE, offering the book to her.)

CHARLOTTE. So now I'm uneducated!

SHAW. There are enough words in my mouth without your putting in more. Can you really have learned so little about me over the past year?

(SHAW puts the book on his desk. CHARLOTTE crosses down left.)

CHARLOTTE. I've learned your High Street demonstrations have a distastefully violent aspect.

SHAW. *(crossing center, above the sofa)* I abhor violence. I cannot simultaneously club a man and cure him. But when standing on a street corner, it is a rhetorical necessity to overstate a case in order to express its importance.

CHARLOTTE. *(crossing to down left of the sofa)* Then what is socialism?

SHAW. It's not posthumous revenge on your mother.

CHARLOTTE. Oh, what a brute you are!

(**CHARLOTTE** *crosses down right.*)

SHAW. Socialism is equality of income, nothing more.

CHARLOTTE. You would turn England into a nation of the poor.

SHAW. I hate the poor: wretched people I wouldn't trust to hold my hat. *(crossing left of the sofa)* – I want to turn England into a nation of people with just enough. If we wish to evolve, we must no longer worship economic gain, but superiority of intellect and dedication toward our fellow creatures.

CHARLOTTE. Superiority of intellect?

SHAW. *(crossing down center)* That special race whose coming Nietzche foretold: the Supermen.

CHARLOTTE. No doubt you count yourself as one of them?

SHAW. Who else?

CHARLOTTE. *(crossing to him)* That's the problem with your theory, Bernie: every man considers himself a Superman. And every woman who wishes to marry must surrender to that delusion.

SHAW. Then perhaps you understand your own predicament a little better.

CHARLOTTE. You have made yourself hateful.

(**BEATRICE** *enters from up right.*)

BEATRICE. Is this a bad time?

SHAW. *(crossing above the sofa to the left)* Ah, Beatrice! Are you mine or Dante's? There is never a bad time to grace us with your presence.

(**CHARLOTTE** *crosses down left.* **SHAW** *moves closer to* **BEATRICE.**)

Trunks packed?

BEATRICE. They're loading the coach. Sidney is seeing to it. Perhaps you could help.

SHAW. Where is it, now? America? New Zealand? Two years without you: How ever will I survive?

BEATRICE. You'll manage.

SHAW. I absolutely hate good-byes. I have never taken the time to see anyone off – not even my mother, who simply packed her things and left – but for my Beatrice – ?

BEATRICE. Do stop.

SHAW. I am yours to command.

*(***SHAW*** grabs the book from the desk and exits, jauntily, up right.)*

CHARLOTTE. He has grown tired of me. What am I to do?

BEATRICE. *(stepping down stage)* The greatest help I can give is to go away. I wanted to leave sooner, but the preparations, the book – It will be better tomorrow when I am gone.

CHARLOTTE. *(moving center, below the sofa)* I wish I could believe you. I've tried everything. I learned to type from his notes and dictation. I live above his office and allow him to visit whenever he needs a rest. I accompany him to the theater, to meals. I insisted we rent this dreadful cottage again to rekindle the magic of last summer. I've even had...intimate relations... I have made myself indispensable to him, yet all I receive in return is callousness.

*(***CHARLOTTE*** sits on the sofa. **BEATRICE** sits beside her.)*

BEATRICE. But Charlotte, a year ago this is what you wanted. You have exclusivity.

CHARLOTTE. He still writes to Ellen Terry.

BEATRICE. Well, as exclusive as Shaw is ever likely to get. Don't you see? You have succeeded.

CHARLOTTE. I have succeeded only in making our every meeting unpleasant. I tell him all the time that he has made himself hateful, when in reality I am the hateful one.

BEATRICE. Why?

CHARLOTTE. Because I am disappointed in myself.

BEATRICE. Whatever for?

CHARLOTTE. *(standing)* For being a more conventional woman than I had thought myself to be. *(crossing down right)* I find socialism interesting less as a political doctrine than as a way of appearing fashionable.

BEATRICE. That's not true.

CHARLOTTE. I couldn't get through your book.

BEATRICE. Neither could the Tories.

(CHARLOTTE crosses above the sofa to up left.)

CHARLOTTE. There are other things. An old melodrama holds my interest better than Ibsen. Wagner? Vegetarianism? Can't bear them. Lately, our only common interest is a dislike of tobacco, and that is hardly the basis for a sound marriage.

BEATRICE. Marriage!

CHARLOTTE. Yes. I've become conventional. I want marriage. It's hopeless.

(CHARLOTTE breaks down. BEATRICE crosses up left to comfort her.)

BEATRICE. Oh, Charlotte. Charlotte, please. If you were really conventional, you'd already be married with children, on an estate in Derry. Convention means doing what is expected.

(BEATRICE leads CHARLOTTE back to the sofa, where they sit.)

In that way, you're only as conventional as Shaw himself. And deep down, he is conventional. You've read his plays.

CHARLOTTE. I read little else.

BEATRICE. Invariably, the main characters make a conventional choice for an unconventional reason. Don't give up hope. There may be a way of convincing Shaw to marry if you could establish an unconventional reason for the convention of marriage.

CHARLOTTE. I love him so much.

BEATRICE. I know, dear.

CHARLOTTE. I've amended my will. He will inherit my estate.

BEATRICE. *(appalled)* Charlotte, what would people think?

CHARLOTTE. They would think the truth. Isn't that what you urge at your school?

BEATRICE. Sidney could get you a ticket to America, if you care to accompany us. You'd be gone for a year, maybe two; long enough to forget all about the great philanderer.

CHARLOTTE. There is no journey long enough for that.

BEATRICE. Long enough for him to forget you.

CHARLOTTE. That is my fear.

BEATRICE. I thought our leaving would help, but now I feel you're being abandoned.

CHARLOTTE. I'd rather you weren't here to witness the breaking of this conventional heart.

(BEATRICE stands, her tone changing.)

BEATRICE. Right. Stand up.

(CHARLOTTE stands.)

Face me. I'm willing to commiserate with misfortune, but I draw the line at self-pitying inaction.

(BEATRICE hands CHARLOTTE a handkerchief.)

Dry your eyes. Your every tear makes him that much stronger. Now formulate a plan.

CHARLOTTE. My plan failed.

BEATRICE. Then formulate another! You are a woman, Charlotte; there's no limit to the weapons in your arsenal. *(crossing down right)* Have you honestly used them all? Or only the ones he's expecting?

CHARLOTTE. I – I don't know.

BEATRICE. *(crossing down left)* Engage him. Remember, he's a sprite. To him, it's a game. Don't play by his rules.

CHARLOTTE. I haven't.

BEATRICE. And look where it's gotten you!

CHARLOTTE. – Nowhere.

BEATRICE. *(triumphantly)* Yes!

CHARLOTTE. I played by my rules and I lost.

BEATRICE. *(more triumphantly)* Yes!

CHARLOTTE. Then should I play by his rules?

BEATRICE. *(most triumphantly)* Yes!

CHARLOTTE. But you're talking in circles.

BEATRICE. Exactly.

> *(**BEATRICE** hugs **CHARLOTTE**, who is still a bit confused.)*

CHARLOTTE. You're a dear friend, Beatrice. I shall miss you.

> *(**CHARLOTTE** gives **BEATRICE** back the handkerchief as **WEBB** enters from up right.)*

WEBB. The coach is all packed.

BEATRICE. Where's Shaw?

WEBB. Having a grand old time unionizing the coachman.

CHARLOTTE. *(to **BEATRICE**)* There may be one more furrow I need to plow – by his rules. – Excuse me.

> *(**CHARLOTTE** exits down left. **WEBB** crosses down right, making a final glance through the room for forgotten objects.)*

BEATRICE. I'm worried about her.

WEBB. Oh?

BEATRICE. Shaw is not treating her well.

WEBB. Oh, yes. Quite. Bad business.

BEATRICE. You must talk to him.

WEBB. Oh, yes. Very – what?

BEATRICE. You must appeal to his honor as a gentleman.

WEBB. Honor as a gentleman? This is Shaw!

BEATRICE. *(crossing to him)* In driving Charlotte away, he is jeopardizing the school and maybe even the Fabian

Society. She is too important to us.

WEBB. *(crossing down left)* What about alienating Shaw? Losing him would be far more detrimental to the cause, not to mention that he is my oldest and closest friend.

BEATRICE. Because he is your friend, you must tell him everything that is wrong with him. *(crossing to him)* – He may listen to you.

WEBB. Yes, but we don't talk about things like that, Bo.

BEATRICE. Do you want to see Charlotte leave Adelphi Terrace and bankrupt the school?

WEBB. You know I don't.

BEATRICE. Then you must talk to Shaw.

(SHAW enters from up right.)

SHAW. Talk to Shaw? About what?

BEATRICE. About unionizing our coachman.

SHAW. The most glorious conversation I've had in weeks! I was sure to point out which of your trunks were too heavy to lift, and how he was being exploited. I was so persuasive that he promised to strike for higher wages between here and the station! *(crossing to the bookcase up left)* …Don't worry, I gave him a copy of your book and told him not to strike until he had read it cover to cover. Based on my estimate of his intellect, the strike won't occur before the twentieth century.

WEBB. Perhaps we should be on our way, then.

BEATRICE. Let me just go through the house one more time.

(BEATRICE starts to exit down right. WEBB follows. She stops.)

You stay with Shaw.

WEBB. Oh.

(BEATRICE exits down right. Pause.)

SHAW. They'll miss you on the council, no doubt.

WEBB. *(crossing center, below the sofa)* It's for a good reason, though.

SHAW. Certainly. Certainly.

(SHAW crosses to his desk to work, but before he can sit, WEBB speaks.)

WEBB. ...Er... How...are things in the vestry?

SHAW. Very interesting, as Charlotte would say. I've written a bill to eliminate the fee for women's public conveniences.

WEBB. *(genuinely interested)* Have you?

SHAW. *(crossing to WEBB)* The men's conveniences have always been free. Why should women be charged a penny?

WEBB. Well done. A penny for most of those poor flower girls is an entire day's wage. Such a fee appears criminal.

SHAW. I'm certain it will pass, so long as I get someone else to introduce it. They don't take any bill I introduce seriously enough to warrant discussion.

WEBB. *(crossing down left)* Yes, well, here's the rub, Shaw. I could go on talking to you all day about women's conveniences, but I feel that, before I leave, I need to broach a sticky subject with you.

SHAW. You're looking more uncomfortable than usual; what is it?

WEBB. Charlotte.

SHAW. Sidney, must we go through this? You are the last person I should have expected to bring this up.

WEBB. That's probably why I was the first one asked.

SHAW. I already know every argument you will make and you already know my every response. There's not a nuance of this issue we haven't already explored in our respective minds.

WEBB. And yet we arrived at different conclusions. *(crossing to SHAW)* – I adore both of you. But when I see the poor woman, how morosely she acts, and how you –

SHAW. How I what?

WEBB. Well, if anyone other than you behaved in such a manner, I would consider it monstrous.

SHAW. But you see, it *is* me, so there is nothing more to discuss.

*(**SHAW** crosses to his desk.)*

WEBB. Bad business, Shaw, extremely –

SHAW. Do you feel I delight in Charlotte's torment? I don't. It pains me. In here. *(his heart)* But in here – *(his head)* I know that our feelings are nothing more than a pleasant distraction from work. Though, over the past few months, they have become decidedly less pleasant.

WEBB. You do Charlotte wrong to call her a distraction.

*(**WEBB** moves to **SHAW**'s desk. **SHAW** counters up left to the bookcase.)*

You're doing three times more work than before. She is your primary helpmate, toiling constantly by your side and asking nothing in return but a kiss a week. What's the difference between that and a marriage? Beatrice and I are just the same: we relish the work, our partnership is more efficient than our individual efforts could ever be, and once a week – well – it is quickly dispatched and we return to what we enjoy.

SHAW. …Once a week?

WEBB. Directly after I wind the clock. …I'm not saying you need to follow our example to the letter! Only recognize that you and Charlotte have become a committee, and that, in truth, pushing her away goes against your beliefs. The central tenet of socialism isn't "every man for himself," it's "join together for the common good." – Put a little effort her way.

SHAW. *(crossing down left)* I do. You know how busy I am. If I am not the busiest man in London, I am a close second to you. *(crossing center, below the sofa)* Yet here I am in Stratford because Charlotte asked me. I devote every second of my spare time to her and she does

nothing but cry and complain and clip my wings. My
nerves are shattered by the scenes of which I have
been made the innocent victim. I wonder is she at all
ashamed of herself. I have allied myself to a fountain
of tears. And yet everyone takes her part.

WEBB. *(crossing to* **SHAW***)* Because they have seen you destroy
so many other women.

SHAW. *(crossing down right)* I destroy no one. They destroy
themselves.

WEBB. Then you have a responsibility to see Charlotte is
not destroyed in such a way. She is not to be lumped
with the others. She is different. And you know she
is different, which is why you are so fond of her. Be
selfish for once. Don't send her away to better the
world. *(crossing to* **SHAW***)* Keep her, and perfect yourself.
– Charlotte may very well be your last, best hope for
the eternal happiness of holy matrimony.

SHAW. Are you by any chance writing a melodrama?

WEBB. Then forget happiness. I'm talking about a partner.

SHAW. *(crossing down left)* No one is up to the task. No
woman has defeated me yet.

WEBB. It's not a struggle for supremacy, it's a recognition
of equality.

SHAW. I have no intention of sharing the glory of Shaw.

WEBB. *(advancing on* **SHAW***)* It is not glorious to abandon
women so cavalierly. It speaks to a flaw in character.
Just because your mother abandoned –

SHAW. *(overlapping after "mother")* I beg your pardon!

WEBB. *(continuing from above)* you when you were younger,
doesn't mean you need to punish every woman –

SHAW. Enough of this! *(***SHAW** *crosses to his desk.)* ...You're
asking me to give Charlotte something she doesn't
want. She does not desire marriage.

WEBB. A woman's desires can change. And if you're not
careful, they will turn into needs.

SHAW. What Charlotte *needs* is to get her mind off me.
Didn't Beatrice once have her in mind for Graham

Wallas? *There's* a wonderful project to pursue.

WEBB. You didn't hear? Wallas is engaged.

SHAW. Well, I'll be damned. Is the date fixed?

WEBB. Ask him. I'll be on the boat.

SHAW. Well, see here, Webb. I thank you for sharing your concerns, but don't wager on my transformation. *(crossing center, below the sofa)* The Superman need not accept the new nexus; he is the new nexus! He not only prefers, he *thrives* upon anarchic and spiritual isolation. But, don't worry, I'll tell Beatrice you gave it your best effort.

WEBB. Thank you, old boy.

(BEATRICE enters from down right.)

BEATRICE. We had better get ready, Sidney. The coachman is getting annoyed.

SHAW. He must read faster than I thought.

WEBB. Have we forgotten anything?

BEATRICE. All packed.

SHAW. *(moving a step or two down left)* Where's Charlotte? I'm sure she will want to say good-bye.

WEBB. I'll get her.

(WEBB exits quickly down left. SHAW and BEATRICE are left alone. Awkward pause.)

BEATRICE. We should probably say our good-byes here.

SHAW. *(crossing down center)* Yes.

(A long, long, painfully long and awkward pause. They do not look each other in the eye. Perhaps SHAW whistles a little. Eventually they establish furtive, peripheral eye contact. They speak simultaneously, but not in unison.)

BOTH. Good-bye.

(WEBB and CHARLOTTE enter from down left.)

WEBB. Here we are.

(WEBB and SHAW shake hands warmly. BEATRICE hugs CHARLOTTE. WEBB takes CHARLOTTE's hand. BEATRICE cannot hug or touch SHAW. The moment

becomes dangerous. **WEBB** *saves her.)*

WEBB. *(cont.)* – Good-bye, then.

*(**WEBB** and **BEATRICE** exit up right. **CHARLOTTE** and **SHAW** are alone.)*

SHAW. Well, that made for a lovely break in the day.

CHARLOTTE. I will miss them.

SHAW. They'll be back. Shall we return to work?

*(**SHAW** sits on the sofa and picks up his galleys.)*

CHARLOTTE. Not just yet.

SHAW. With your permission, I'll plunge right in. I'm afraid I haven't time to waste.

CHARLOTTE. It's Saturday, you know.

SHAW. So it is.

CHARLOTTE. Something happens on Saturday.

SHAW. Hm? Oh, yes. Come to collect your weekly wage, have you? Very well. Come here.

*(**SHAW** stands. **CHARLOTTE** crosses to him. **SHAW** bends to kiss her lightly. She holds his head and attempts to make the kiss passionate.)*

There now. That out of the way? Let's get back to work.

*(**SHAW** sits. **CHARLOTTE** crosses down right.)*

CHARLOTTE. I like that we don't operate under a conventional wage scheme.

SHAW. It makes it easier to balance the books, certainly.

CHARLOTTE. I may not say it as often as I should anymore, but – I enjoy being unconventional with you.

SHAW. *(an attempt at tenderness)* It is a feeling I return, unequivocally.

CHARLOTTE. In fact, I need to ask you rather an unconventional question. At once. And I'll need an answer before I return to work.

SHAW. *(amused)* Very well.

CHARLOTTE. …Would you marry me?

(Pause. **SHAW** *looks at* **CHARLOTTE** *as though seeing her for the first time.)*

I know how much you despise convention. What's more unconventional than a woman proposing to a man?

SHAW. Charlotte, you tumble beneath me with such a question. You become like all of the others. I thought you the superwoman, committed to independence and equality.

CHARLOTTE. Sometimes it is a rhetorical necessity to overstate a case in order to express its importance.

SHAW. *(standing)* My dear green-eyed one, we so rarely share a warm moment anymore. Must the warmth again turn heated? *(crossing to her, tenderly)* My answer is no. The only rational response to such a question is no. *(crossing to the sofa)* …I'd rather follow the Webbs to Australia.

CHARLOTTE. Why?

SHAW. Because I care for you.

(She crosses up right, frustrated.)

I care for you too deeply to condemn you to such a horrible institution.

CHARLOTTE. It is not a condemnation; I desire it.

SHAW. Of course you do, *now*. Because you are addled by your heart. The best argument against marriage is that it is a lifetime contract made upon a temporary stirring of the emotions.

CHARLOTTE. My emotions are not temporary.

SHAW. *(crossing up left)* All emotions are temporary. Marriage is forever; and forever lasts longer than a rash promise made upon a broken heart.

CHARLOTTE. *(moving to him)* You don't think we could be happy together for all eternity?

SHAW. If I smile for a mere ten minutes, my cheeks hurt; how could I be expected to remain cheerful for eternity? Eternity is what makes marriage unbearable.

CHARLOTTE. *(crossing down left)* But what else is there? I will play by your rules. If not marriage, what? If not for eternity, for how long?

SHAW. I would propose that marriage become a series of renewable one year contracts.

CHARLOTTE. Don't mock me.

SHAW. *(crossing up right)* Tell someone he will be condemned to something forever, and he will exert all of his will to escape. Tell that same someone he will only be permitted a certain pleasure for a short period, and he will exert all of his will to prolong it. The fear of losing the loved one on the anniversary of the contract would keep everyone together and on their best behavior.

CHARLOTTE. *(crossing down right)* I'm not interested in the marriage of everyone. I am talking about us.

SHAW. *(crossing up left)* But we are a part of the greater society. You wouldn't cross a bridge that's falling down. You would fix it first.

CHARLOTTE. *(crossing center, above the sofa)* But you would fix it with your hands, not hot air. Marriage will never be renewable contracts.

SHAW. *(crossing down left)* No, but you'd get a similar effect if the divorce laws were so extended that a marriage could be dissolved as easily as a business partnership: in fact most marriages would be "only for a year, mind," and would last a lifetime.

CHARLOTTE. Would you marry me for only a year, then?

SHAW. Until the laws are changed, I don't see how. Naturally, the old system still has the support of women because they are not economically independent of men.

*(**SHAW** crosses to his desk. **CHARLOTTE** meets him there.)*

CHARLOTTE. I am.

SHAW. *(returning to down left)* Until you have a husband, at which point he controls your property. Under present conditions, women must choose between the illicit exchange of sex for money found in the streets, and the socially-accepted, church-sanctioned version of the same exchange which we call marriage.

CHARLOTTE. I would not be prostituting myself in marrying you.

SHAW. But you *would* be making a bad match.

CHARLOTTE. *(crossing center, below the sofa)* Do you think I am only proposing to you because you haven't a shilling?

SHAW. I am merely pointing out the very real difference in our incomes.

CHARLOTTE. – Do you mean to say that *you* would be the one who is prostituted!?

SHAW. Consider the situation: I would lose all authority as a socialist reformer.

CHARLOTTE. *(stepping toward him)* How dare you! Bernie, how dare you say such a thing to me!

SHAW. If I were to stand on High Street deriding the rich, while harboring a wealthy spouse, I would not stand a chance of converting anyone to the cause. I would be all that I claim to rebel against.

*(**SHAW** crosses down right.)*

CHARLOTTE. But look at the Webbs, they're exactly the same as you and I. More so. Sidney comes from a lower class than you, and Beatrice comes from a higher class than I. They bridged farther extremes than we would need to cross, and nobody thinks less of them.

SHAW. *(crossing to his desk)* But Beatrice makes up for her wealth through a single-minded devotion to the cause, a devotion you could never match.

CHARLOTTE. *(crossing to center, below the sofa)* Would you prefer to marry someone like Beatrice?

SHAW. *(exploding)* I would prefer to marry no one! I have repeated this continually since we first met. We sat on this very sofa and swore never to marry. I intend to honor what I have sworn. If you have changed your mind and are eager to marry, then I encourage you to do so.

CHARLOTTE. You encourage me to do so just as often as you encourage me *not* to do so. How can I follow your advice if it goes in circles?

SHAW. *(crossing to her)* My only advice is not to marry me. Follow that, and we will both be happy.

CHARLOTTE. But I love you! Bernie, you make me so miserable!

SHAW. *(returning to his desk)* I have warned you not to clip my wings. If you love me, you will let me soar. You must leave, find work, separate from me.

CHARLOTTE.. *(moving to him)* Such talk only makes me want to draw closer to you. You know that, that's why you say it. You delight in torturing me.

(SHAW advances on her in sarcastic fury, forcing her to retreat to the sofa over the following.)

SHAW. Then stay! Never leave me! Smother me with wild, passionate kisses! Is that what you want to hear?

CHARLOTTE. You are hateful! God, you are a brute to mock me so!

(CHARLOTTE collapses on the sofa. A pause as she weeps. SHAW offers his handkerchief. CHARLOTTE accepts. SHAW speaks as kindly as he can manage.)

SHAW. Forgive me. I never mean to be cruel. …I have an iron ring around my chest, which tightens and grips my heart when I think that you are tormented. Loosen it, oh ever dear to me, by a word to say that you forgive me. Or else lend me my fare to Australia, to Siberia, to the mountains of the moon, to any place where I can torment nobody but myself. I am sorry – not vainly sorry; but painfully, wistfully, affectionately sorry that you are hurt; but if you could see my mind you would not be hurt. I am so certain of that that I am in violently brutally high spirits in spite of that iron ring.

CHARLOTTE. *(returning the handkerchief)* Thank you.

SHAW. *(crossing to his desk)* If you like, I could nominate you for the Fabian executive. We could work side by side.

CHARLOTTE. That will not be necessary. …Good-bye.

(CHARLOTTE stands and grabs her coat and hat from

the hook down left.)

SHAW. Where are you going?

CHARLOTTE. Away.

SHAW. Where away?

CHARLOTTE. Away from you, as you suggested.

SHAW. But what about all of my work? I need to proofread the galleys of the book. There are prefaces and reviews to be typed. Who will take care of them?

CHARLOTTE. I am setting you free, Bernie, to soar with unclipped wings; to do the work yourself.

*(**SHAW** crosses down center.)*

SHAW. Yes, that's splendid! Nobody enjoys a joke more than I, but now let's return to –

CHARLOTTE. Good-bye, Bernie.

*(**CHARLOTTE** starts to exit down left.)*

SHAW. Yes, all right, it's over now.

CHARLOTTE. *(Returning in fury, right in his face)* What is over is your domination over me. If you wish to torture me further, you'll have to marry me first.

*(**CHARLOTTE** exits down left. **SHAW** laughs as the lights fade and the scene change music begins.)*

Scene 2

(The stage is divided into different areas. Center is **SHAW***'s desk at his home office in Fitzroy Square. Beside the desk is a large waste paper basket. Atop the desk is a bowl of oatmeal. Surrounding the desk area are four pools of light, which rise or diminish as people enter and exit them.* **SHAW** *is at his desk as the lights come up. He speaks out. As* **SHAW** *speaks,* **CHARLOTTE** *enters the pool of light down left.)*

SHAW. July, 1897. My dearest Charlotte,
The iron ring has been clutching me bitterly since last we spoke. Hasten to ease it a little. Write something happy.

*(***BEATRICE*** enters the down right pool of light as* **CHARLOTTE** *speaks.)*

CHARLOTTE. Dear Beatrice,
I have decided upon a Fabian approach and am leaving Bernie to his period of anarchic spiritual isolation. Do you have any advice for me?

*(***WEBB*** enters the up right pool of light as* **BEATRICE** *speaks.)*

BEATRICE. How nice to see our theories put into practice. Sidney will provide you with the tools.

*(***BEATRICE*** exits as* **WEBB** *speaks.)*

WEBB. Keep him isolated. And don't force him into a decision. Let him make the discovery himself.

SHAW. Charlotte, it is most inconvenient having Adelphi Terrace shut up. I'm forced to work at my mother's. Haven't spoken to a soul (except in vestry) all week.

WEBB. He will be angry.

SHAW. The hellborn printer has not sent the proof! Damn the printer – blast him, curse him, burn him, double-damn him! It is so lonely, cursing all by myself.

WEBB. He will use emotional manipulation.

SHAW. If you don't come home, I shall go straight down to the Embankment and plunge into the flood.

WEBB. But he must stew in his juices of isolation until the benefits of the new social organization become clear. This is the first method of the Fabians: gradualism.

*(Lights down on **WEBB** as he exits. **CHARLOTTE** has moved to the up left pool of light over **WEBB**'s last sentence. Irish music is heard.)*

CHARLOTTE. Bernie, I am spending September with my sister in Ireland. If you need to reach me, the address is enclosed.

*(Music fades. Pool of light rises up right. **CHARLOTTE** moves to it during **SHAW**'s line.)*

SHAW. I have nowhere to go, nobody to talk to. Lonely – no, by God, never – *not* lonely, but detestably deserted.

*(**SHAW** begins to eat from the bowl of oatmeal. French music plays underneath.)*

CHARLOTTE. Paris is lovely in autumn. I'm sorry you're so alone. I too feel a twinge and have hit upon the perfect solution. ...A poodle!

SHAW. *(nearly choking on the oatmeal)* Not a poodle! If I am to have a rival, let him be at least human.

*(**SHAW** puts the bowl down.)*

CHARLOTTE. November already. It must be dreadful – alone in London, with no one beside you for warmth.

SHAW. Rubbish!

*(**SHAW** removes a shawl from the desk and dons it over the following.)*

CHARLOTTE. I knitted the enclosed shawl for you.

SHAW. Thanks for the shawl. I caught about seventeen separate colds since you left.

*(**SHAW** sneezes.)*

I contemplate nature a shivering wreck.

(French music fades. Lights dim on **SHAW** *as a pool of light rises on* **WEBB** *up left. He holds a bowl of congealed oatmeal.)*

WEBB. Permeation is the second tool of the Fabians. It is the means by which we overcome the supposed threat that new ideas may engender.

*(***WEBB*** places the bowl of oatmeal on the stage, outside the pool of light, nearest* **SHAW***, as the lights arise on* **BEATRICE** *in the down left pool. She too carries a bowl of congealed oatmeal.)*

BEATRICE. We must bombard him with arguments in favor of the new nexus.

*(***BEATRICE*** places her bowl on the ground outside her pool of light nearest* **SHAW** *as* **WEBB** *speaks.)*

WEBB. In this way the ideas appear more common and popular.

(Lights down on **WEBB** *and* **CHARLOTTE** *as the lights come up on* **SHAW***. As* **BEATRICE** *speaks,* **WEBB** *enters her pool of light and they put their arms around each other. Romantic, pastoral, American music plays in the background.)*

BEATRICE. Ah, Shaw: Lecturing in America has been extraordinarily stimulating. The *companionship* has been *delightful.* Our married life is like the early summer, growth and the delight in growing, love and the delight in loving.

SHAW. Drivel!

BEATRICE. How full with happiness human life can be.

SHAW. I can't bear anymore!

(American music fades. **SHAW** *turns upstage as the lights dim on him. Lights come up on* **CHARLOTTE** *down right, ostensibly now in England. Appropriate music is heard.)*

CHARLOTTE. Arrived in Radlett, where I am staying with Lion Phillimore. *She* has extended you an invitation.

(A crash is heard, followed immediately by a cry from **SHAW**. *Music fades.* **SHAW** *turns downstage as the lights come up to reveal a sling on his left arm.)*

SHAW. I scraped the road with my left arm on the way to Radlett.

*(**CHARLOTTE** gasps and moves toward **SHAW**.)*

BEATRICE. Charlotte, no.

CHARLOTTE. But he's hurt.

SHAW. You need to come down to London.

WEBB. It's a game.

*(**CHARLOTTE** is drawn to **SHAW**, who relishes it.)*

SHAW. I know you can't keep away forever. It's too painful for you.

BEATRICE. Charlotte – !

*(**CHARLOTTE** collects herself.)*

CHARLOTTE. I'm leaving Radlett. Mrs. Phillimore has invited me to accompany her to Dieppe.

WEBB. Well done, Charlotte. Leave him isolated.

*(**WEBB** and **BEATRICE** exit as their light fades.)*

SHAW. What the devil is in Dieppe?

CHARLOTTE. *I* will be in Dieppe.

SHAW. And you expect me to drop my work and come along? No, thank you. I bar the seaside a trois. You will resume your secretarial duties tomorrow.

CHARLOTTE. I will not.

*(**CHARLOTTE** crosses resolutely to the rising pool of light down left. The pool she exited fades. French music.)*

I am an independent and unencumbered woman. – Greetings from Dieppe!

SHAW. *(exploding)* What do you mean by this inconceivable conduct?

CHARLOTTE. *(exploding back)* I told you the terms of my return quite clearly last summer. The next time you see me, you had better be on one knee!

SHAW. Go, then, ungrateful wretch: have your heart's desire: find a Master – one who will spend your money, and rule in your house!

(Music fades and lights fade on SHAW, as a pool of light rises up right, revealing WEBB.)

WEBB. Obviously, some subjects accept the new nexus more gradually than others.

CHARLOTTE. This is not gradual; it's glacial. We need a new tack. Try permeation.

WEBB. We are permeating.

CHARLOTTE. Isolation, then.

WEBB. He's isolated.

CHARLOTTE. Then give me complete immobility!

WEBB. Charlotte, please.

CHARLOTTE. Broken bones!

WEBB. I can't –

CHARLOTTE. Give me all the powers of hell!

WEBB. I'm just an economist!

(WEBB's light fades as SHAW's light rises. SHAW holds his forehead.)

SHAW. My head is splitting with neuralgia. Why have you stopped writing? Are there no stamps? Has the post been abolished?

(SHAW turns upstage and his light fades. Light rises on BEATRICE down right. BEATRICE holds another bowl of congealed oatmeal, which she places on the stage as CHARLOTTE speaks.)

CHARLOTTE. Give me an occupation. Anything to distract my mind. If I cannot be indispensable to him, I must become indispensable to myself.

BEATRICE. Go to Rome. Research the municipal and social conditions.

(Lights on BEATRICE and CHARLOTTE fade as the light on SHAW rises. SHAW turns downstage with a

swollen cheek and a bandage tied longitudinally around his head. He still wears the sling.)

SHAW. I discovered the reason for my neuralgia: an impacted tooth. What with that and the feverish healing of my lacerated gum, I am in a most hypochondriacal state. Why do you choose this time of all others to desert me – just now when you are most wanted?

(Lights on **CHARLOTTE** *up left. Italian music.)*

CHARLOTTE. You told me to go away, and I have. You told me to make myself useful, and I am. If you have any other advice you'd care for me to follow, the hotel address is enclosed.

SHAW. How nice to hear from you after all this time, but I'm afraid you are too late. Your services as secretary are no longer required, due to the unexpected appearance of Mrs. Kate Salt. In the absence of sentimental interruptions we get along famously.

CHARLOTTE. Rome is proving more interesting than I imagined.

SHAW. Haste to attack the Roman municipal problem; for there is clearly no future for you as a secretary.

*(***SHAW*** turns upstage.)*

CHARLOTTE. I feel the subject requires a whole book. Who knows if I shall ever return!

(Italian music fades. Small crash. **SHAW** *winces and rubs his head as he turns downstage.)*

SHAW. I broke my head with a Shannon file. Oh, Charlotte, Charlotte, is this a time to be gadding about in Rome.

*(***SHAW*** turns upstage as his light fades. Lights rise on* **BEATRICE** *up right. She holds another bowl of congealed oatmeal and places it on the stage as* **CHARLOTTE** *speaks.)*

CHARLOTTE. Rome! Beatrice, there is much for us to learn here. As I observe and explore the city's life, both high and low, there are moments when my own private torment is subsumed by the suffering of those I see around me.

(Lights up on **SHAW**, *who turns turns downstage, scratching himself. Lights down on the women.)*

SHAW. Now, to add to my other woes, I have developed nettle rash and am slathered from head to toe with ointments and unguents.

(Lights on **WEBB** *down left, who carries a stack of old books.)*

WEBB. I begin to worry about Charlotte –

SHAW. *Et tu,* Sidney? Have pity. I live the life of a dog.

(Lights down on the men. Lights up on the women. **WEBB** *places his stack of books on the stage. Italian music again.)*

CHARLOTTE. But lately, Beatrice, that fog of common suffering dissipates into a world-encompassing glow of satisfaction, knowing that the work I'm doing can make a difference in the lives of so many. Is this what you and Sidney feel when you speak of dedication? Is it for this that Bernie sent me away? If so, I now understand.

(Lights down on **CHARLOTTE**. *Music fades. Lights up on the men.)*

BEATRICE. Charlotte no longer needs you, Shaw; she's become everything you claim to desire. Yet I believe she still loves you. I shouldn't be surprised if you marry her after all.

SHAW. She has given up writing to me.

*(***BEATRICE** *enters* **WEBB**'s *light as he speaks. Her pool diminishes.)*

WEBB. There is a solution, my old friend: Return from your period of anarchic spiritual isolation. Accept the new nexus, as we have.

(WEBB and BEATRICE kiss and exit arm in arm. Their light fades. SHAW takes off his shoe and stands over the following. CHARLOTTE's light rises up left.)

SHAW. If only you could see me. While riding home from Ealing, I find my left foot unaccountably sore. On taking off the shoe, my foot expands to the size of a leg of mutton.

(SHAW sticks his left foot into the trash can. He shouts in pain and lifts his leg out of the trash can to reveal that it is swathed in bandages. He still wears the sling and toothache bandage. He sits and puts his injured foot on the desk.)

Locomotion is now very excruciating. I am completely immobile, my bones broken. Are all the powers of hell against me?

CHARLOTTE. Very interesting! If it is really as you say, then I shall return to London. I shall arrive on May Day.

SHAW. At last! I shall hop down to Victoria Station and greet you!

CHARLOTTE. No. Remain immobile. I will see you at home. – We have much to discuss.

(Triumphant music plays. SHAW leans back happily as paper rains from the skies, covering the stage. The lights fade.)

Scene 3

(SHAW's room at his mother's house in Fitzroy Square. It is a mess, littered with opened books, crumpled and strewn paper, and congealed, half-eaten bowls of oatmeal. Somewhere within this mess is SHAW's desk, upon which he has cleared a small semicircle of uncluttered work space. SHAW sits in his chair, facing away from the desk. The only bandage remaining is the one on his left foot. The injured leg is elevated. He is writing in a tablet. There is a tentative knock on the door. Pause. Another knock, louder.)

SHAW. Come.

(CHARLOTTE enters from down right.)

CHARLOTTE. Hello, Bernie. How are you feeling?

(SHAW puts the tablet down.)

SHAW. Has the prodigal lover returned?

CHARLOTTE. I asked after your foot, not your heart. How are you feeling?

SHAW. Like the popes in Dante. – In truth, the lack of movement is the best thing ever to happen to me. Being nailed to this chair has allowed me to devote all my energy toward the new play: *Caesar and Cleopatra*: how it will infuriate everyone!

CHARLOTTE. *(smiling)* You change every adversity into an advantage. I missed that kind of optimism when I was away.

SHAW. It was always here.

(an awkward pause)

CHARLOTTE. Have you nothing to ask me – ?

SHAW. I do: – How was Rome?

CHARLOTTE. That's not the question I wanted, Bernie. I won't play games with you, arguing over theoretical concepts. I'm not that woman anymore. I'm here to work.

SHAW. And that's why I asked you about Italy. If I were playing a game, I'd recount for you a daily almanac of my horrid suffering in your absence. But I made no mention of it at all, until you brought it up.

CHARLOTTE. I won't play, Bernie. My departure hurt us both. The difference is: you have the power to ease that suffering with a single question.

(a curmudgeon-silencing beat)

SHAW. Was the research productive?

CHARLOTTE. It – Oh, Bernie, it was transformative. *(moving into the room for the first time)* Joining into the common human struggle for the first time in my life, I felt vital. *(crossing down left)* Not sitting in a tower, drawing conclusions about a world I'd never seen. But being there, at the source of the problem, and discovering practical solutions. *(She is beside him.)* I work now. I've enough material for a book of my own.

SHAW. What form will it take? Some thrilling memoir that gives the whole history of a lady of quality suffering from a broken heart – giving full particulars – and being rescued from herself by the call of public work?

CHARLOTTE. No.

(a beat)

SHAW. …You no longer laugh at my jokes.

CHARLOTTE. I came to see how you are recovering. If my other business will not be addressed, I shall be leaving.

*(**CHARLOTTE** starts to exit down right. **SHAW** stops her verbally.)*

SHAW. – Have pity, Charlotte. Don't go. Look what has become of me. My very existence hangs by a thread.

CHARLOTTE. Your existence does not hang by a thread.

SHAW. It does. The toe isn't healing. It's abscessed. I need it drained and scraped by a surgeon, but can't afford the operation. Look at my desk; the petrified bowls of oatmeal; this is how I have lived for the past two months.

CHARLOTTE. Life will return to normal once your mother returns.

SHAW. Returns from where?

CHARLOTTE. From wherever she is.

SHAW. She's downstairs.

CHARLOTTE. I assumed from this mess that she had gone away.

SHAW. Good heavens, no. She's always here, she simply ignores me. It's how she has treated me since the day I was born.

CHARLOTTE. …This is monstrous!

SHAW. *(delighted at the change in tone)* Indeed it is!

CHARLOTTE. *(crossing down left)* For a woman to ignore her own son!

SHAW. *Invalid* son!

CHARLOTTE. *Invalid* son. It's positively criminal!

SHAW. Hear hear!

CHARLOTTE. *(crossing to him)* Your toe isn't healing!

SHAW. Precisely.

CHARLOTTE. It's abscessed!

SHAW. Exactly!

CHARLOTTE. It needs to be drained and scraped!

SHAW. Oh, this is much better.

CHARLOTTE. I shall give her a good dressing down.

(CHARLOTTE starts to exit again. SHAW stops her.)

SHAW. No no no no no no no no no. It's impossible. There are two things Mother cannot ever be: dressed down and dressed up. You'd be the Christian before the lions.

CHARLOTTE. It's outrageous.

SHAW. I have come to accept it. *(SHAW hops left, sitting forlornly.)* – Eventually I am neglected by *all* the women who are dear to me.

CHARLOTTE. *(crossing to him)* Except for your mother, no woman neglects you. You send them away.

SHAW. *(grabbing her hand)* And why should you want to be like them? Stay! And nurse me back to health! What better work for the cause can there be?

CHARLOTTE. *(pulling her hand free)* What about Rome?

SHAW. *(clearing a space for her on the desk)* Write it here. With my assistance, it will be built in a day.

CHARLOTTE. You shall become *my* secretary then?

SHAW. Certainly not. If you wish to take care of me, you must suggest a different arrangement.

CHARLOTTE. If you would like to be taken care of, *you* must suggest the arrangement. My choice is already established.

(SHAW sits at the desk.)

SHAW. Marriage is not an acceptable alternative. It is an abomination and a nightmare.

CHARLOTTE. The same optimism that leads you to consider a bandaged foot a blessing, can lead you to good conclusions about marriage.

SHAW. You're saying I should consider marriage as pleasant as an infected toe.

CHARLOTTE. I'm saying that if the theory doesn't work in practice, it needs to change. Just as I have changed. You think I'm here for sentimental reasons? My beliefs in marriage are the opposite of what they were.

SHAW. You still want to marry! Your beliefs are the opposite, and yet the same. Perhaps you're confusing belief with opportunity.

CHARLOTTE. Get off your horse, Bernie. I've entertained a suitor in my time. A woman of means never lacks for marital opportunity.

SHAW. I don't mean Dr. Munthe.

CHARLOTTE. *(crossing down right, away from him)* And neither do I.

SHAW. Damnation! Who was he?

CHARLOTTE. *(turning to him)* Count Sponnek.

SHAW. Count who?

CHARLOTTE. It doesn't matter, he went back to Russia. … there was also J. S. Black…

SHAW. More than one?! Damnation!

CHARLOTTE. *(crossing down left)* Finch Hutton. Herbert Oakley. Arthur Smith-Barry.

SHAW. Is that all?

CHARLOTTE. *(crossing up left)* That I can remember by name. There was also an army major, a general, a major general –

SHAW. Good God, I can't listen to any more.

CHARLOTTE. It stings, doesn't it. But you are the one I have chosen.

SHAW. I have built myself a tower, that no one can assail. If I marry you, I crumble.

CHARLOTTE. *(crossing behind him)* You're crumbling now, alone. Marriage is the support that allows that tower to grow ever higher. If the Superman needs to set an example, why can't he do it through the super-marriage?

SHAW. *(a glimpse beneath the veneer)* …you could live without romance? Eternal happiness?

CHARLOTTE. I've given up on eternal happiness with you, Bernie. I'm holding out for ten minutes quiet. *(beside him)* As for romance, we had our fair share that first summer. Three months of lies and laughter. Let us return to the struggle for survival.

SHAW. I could never subject you to the subservience – .

CHARLOTTE. *(crossing down right)* Bother the subservience! That's last year's argument. And it's precisely why you will make a good husband. – I shall ask again, if it makes you uncomfortable: will you marry me?

*(**SHAW** winces. A pause. He wrestles with his soul.)*

SHAW. I can't.

CHARLOTTE. Why not?

SHAW. Because the subject makes me emotional! – The fea
– the *thought* of what may result from this discussion…
It drives my passions to the fore. Softening my mind –
I feel them do it – forcing me into a deci – a foolhardy
decision, which I will reject with all my strength.

CHARLOTTE. *(crossing to him)* You don't have to reject it.

SHAW. I do reject it! Romance is not a reason! I need *words*,
Charlotte. I need *debate.*

CHARLOTTE. Debate is your excuse to avoid action.

SHAW. Debate *is* action.

CHARLOTTE. *Decision* is action.

SHAW. *(standing)* I've made my decision. It's you who must
force me out of it. You can only defeat me with the
shock of the unconventional.

CHARLOTTE. *(crossing down left)* Oh, you are infuriating! I
have no intention of defeating you. I have not tried
to bring you down the last ten months, I have tried to
raise myself up.

SHAW. But marriage is defeat.

CHARLOTTE. No, Bernie. Defeat is refusing to ride life's
bicycle. – Marry me, or say goodbye.

SHAW. Goodbye.

(Pause. **CHARLOTTE** *is devastated.)*

CHARLOTTE. Very well.

(She crosses to the door down right.)

SHAW. Don't go.

*(She turns to him in anticipation. Pause. He tries to
speak, but cannot form the words.)*

CHARLOTTE. What are you trying to say?

SHAW. …I –

CHARLOTTE. Go on.

SHAW. I –

CHARLOTTE. Yes?

*(***SHAW*** deflates.)*

CHARLOTTE. *(cont.)* Don't stop now, Bernie. Your silence is more eloquent than ten pages of debate.

(**SHAW** *looks at her helplessly. Beat.*)

Do you love me?

(His look indicates the affirmative.)

I love you too.

(She embraces and comforts him. He returns the affection unreservedly.)

Forget the words, Bernie. Give in to your emotions. We'll be married now, won't we.

SHAW. No.

CHARLOTTE. What???

SHAW. I only asked you to stay. You must change my mind, not my feelings.

CHARLOTTE. *(crossing left)* What else can I do? I've tried every tool a woman could possibly employ and it wasn't good enough. – I give up.

SHAW. You can't surrender! The Superwoman never surrenders. She lives for the struggle to attain the unattainable!

CHARLOTTE. Put a stopper in it for once.

(**SHAW** *grabs her in his arms.*)

SHAW. I won't let you diminish yourself in this way.

CHARLOTTE. What are you doing?

SHAW. Marry me!

CHARLOTTE. Bernie!

SHAW. It's the only thing that can save you from abdicating your responsibility to the Life Force!

CHARLOTTE. – Do you mean it?

SHAW. I do.

CHARLOTTE. I will marry you, Bernard Shaw. Though I may never understand the reason why.

SHAW. Agreed?

CHARLOTTE. Agreed.

SHAW. …What about sex?

(They separate. Victorian propriety returns.)

CHARLOTTE. …I assumed that, having experienced it together once, we'd need not experience it again.

SHAW. I suppose it is never again as magical as the first time –

CHARLOTTE. Disappointing news indeed.

SHAW. As a gesture of equality, I could let you determine where and when we – wind the clock.

CHARLOTTE. The result would be the same.

SHAW. But the Life Force in its effort to create the Superman – !

CHARLOTTE. If the Life Force intended you to sire the Superman, it would not have led you to such an ordinary, middle-aged woman as I.

SHAW. But sex and the desire for conjugation – !

CHARLOTTE. Conjugation has nothing to do with marriage, Bernie; it is an incidental consequence of it. Two separate strangers coupling and having a child are not considered husband and wife; but two people sharing the same domestic situation without sex or children are. It is domesticity that makes a marriage.

SHAW. *(anagnorisis, worthy of the Ancient Greeks)* By God, you're right! How wonderfully unconventional! It has been staring me in the face all my life, and I never saw it before! Marriage is not a sexual contract, but a social one! And man is a social animal! – You're the most extraordinary woman I have ever met.

CHARLOTTE. That took far longer than expected.

SHAW. Nevertheless, may I bow to convention and kiss you again?

CHARLOTTE. Bernie: I'm to be your wife, not your secretary.

*(**CHARLOTTE** extends her hand. **SHAW** takes it politely.)*

SHAW. I had expected more of –

*(**CHARLOTTE** puts a finger over his lips. She speaks gently.)*

CHARLOTTE. Ten minutes.

SHAW. But –

CHARLOTTE. Please.

SHAW. We –

CHARLOTTE. Shh.

(They smile. Pause. Music starts. Slowly, gradually, almost imperceptibly at first, the handshake becomes an awkward, then a comfortable embrace. Curtain.)

COSTUME PLOT

Sidney Webb

Act I - 1
    brown suit
    brown waistcoat
    tie
    shirt
    pince nez
    brown shoes
    collar
    undershirt

I - 2
    same

I - 3
    same

Act II - 1
    grey suit
    waistcoat
    tie
    grey overcoat
    black bowler hat
    pince nez
    shirt
    collar

II - 2
    same suit
    no hat
    no coat

Beatrice Webb

Act I - 1
    peach suit
    blouse
    corset
    tights
    blackboots
    cameo
    camisol

I - 2
    same
    add shawl

I - 3
    same
    add capelet
    handbag
    hat

Act II - 1
    brown plaid dress
    burgundy overcoat
    hat
    handbag

II - 2
    same
    no outer wear
    no hat

Shaw

Act I - 1
    ochre Norfolk jacket
    collarless shirt
    brown pants
    cap

I - 2
    same

I - 3
    same

Act II - 1
    brown jacket
    green waistcoat
    tie
    henley undershirt
    handkerchief

II - 2
    same
    no jacket
    add sling and "plaster" on cheek
    add head bandage - no tie
    add bandage for foot - unbutton shirt
    no collar

II - 3
    same
    just bandage on foot
    walking stick

Charlotte

Act I- 1
- red & beige suit
- plaid shirt
- hat
- tights w/ rip
- black boots
- corset
- camisol

I - 2
- same
- no jacket
- no hat

I - 3
- same
- add shawl

Act II - 1
- green skirt
- striped jacket
- cream blouse
- cameo
- tights
- black boots
- camisol

II - 2
- add capalet as muff
- add fur capelet
- add peach capelet
- add hat - Dieppe
- add grey shawl w/ black lace - Italy

II - 3
- same

MUSIC CUES

1. Lights out into Act I Scene 1

2. Scene change to Scene 2

3. Scene change to scene 3

4. End of Act I

5. Lights out into Act II Scene 1

6. Scene change to Scene 2

7. Irish - pennywhistle

8. Paris - accordion

9. Dieppe - accordion

10. Rome - accordion/mandolin

11. End of Act II / Bows

SET DESIGNS

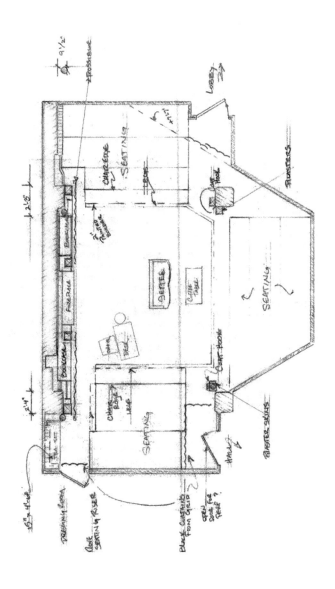

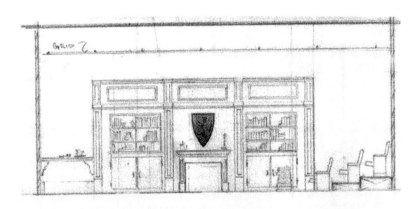

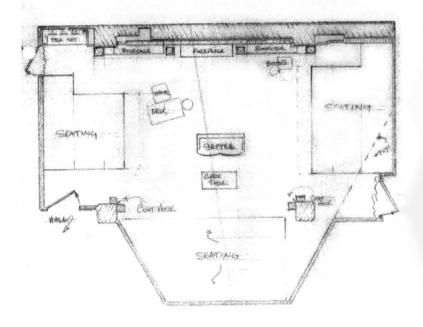

PROPERTY PLOT

Act I

Preset:

    settee

        on settee: small pillow

    coffee table

    desk

        on desk: bill ledger

        stack of envelopes

        piles of papers

        various bills

        "Matchmaker journal"

        letter opener

        fountain pen

        Quintessence of Isbenism

    chair - at desk

    wastebasket - with crumpled paper inside

    Fabian Society shield - hanging over fireplace

    Victorian tea service - teapot, 2-3 cups/saucers, creamer pot, sugar
        bowl, tongs

    sugar cubes - consumable

    typewriter - practical

    books on stage left shelves

Offstage:

    parcel with beefsteak

    The Philanderer galley

    wooden crate

        in crate: "The Snake in the Grass" painting

    knife

    claw to open crate

    cigarette case

    leaves - on Shaw as he enters, removed offstage

Act II

Preset:

    desk:

        on desk: public conveniences bill

        Shaw's journal

    Shaw's writing tablet - on stage left bookshelf

Personal:

    Handkerchief

    oatmeal bowls

    cover for couch

    arm sling

    head bandage

    foot bandage

CPSIA information can be obtained
at www.ICGtesting.com
Printed in the USA
LVHW051457051118
596010LV00011B/589/P